Maryland
State Facts

Nickname:	Old Line State
Date Entered Union:	April 28, 1788 (the 7th state)
Motto:	*Fatti maschil parole femine* (Manly deeds, womanly words)
Famous Maryland Men:	Spiro T. Agnew, *former U.S. vice president* Frederick Douglass, *abolitionist* Johns Hopkins, *financier* Babe Ruth, *baseball player* Frank Zappa, *musician*
Bird:	Baltimore oriole
Flower:	Black-eyed Susan
Fact:	The United States Naval Academy is located in Annapolis, Maryland.

My darling Ben,

This is surely the craziest-sounding letter you've ever received but please, please, I'm begging you to read the whole thing, for the sake of our precious Jenny if not for me.

I don't have a clue where to start. The beginning makes no more sense than the rest of it. I didn't die in the accident. I mean, part of me did. The physical part. But the rest, the real me, didn't. The Real Me is still living in the body of Marina Devereaux—

Carrie threw the pen across the elegant living room. It hit the wall and clattered to the polished hardwood floor. "How can you explain the impossible?" she asked aloud.

Rising, she tore the unfinished letter into small shreds and stuffed it into the trash compactor in the neat little kitchen. As she did, the Realtor's magazine on the counter caught her eye and she slowly reached for it. There. On the fourth page. It was a nice enough house. She should know. She'd lived next door to it…when she was Carrie.

She eyed the phone. Was she insane even to be thinking about moving into a house next door to her husband and baby? Tears stung her eyes. She was so desperately hungry for the sight of her family. It might be enough simply to live close by, to catch glimpses of them each day, to know they were healthy and coping. It would *have* to be enough, she amended. Ben would never believe her if she tried to tell him who she was.

She reached for the phone with her jaw set in determination. He sister Jillian would be glad to go with her. Marina Kerr Devereaux intended to get a contract on that house *today*.

American
HEROES
AGAINST ALL ODDS

ANNE MARIE
WINSTON

Chance at a Lifetime

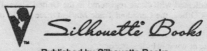

Silhouette Books

Published by Silhouette Books

America's Publisher of Contemporary Romance

For Karen Rose Smith,
whose gentle encouragement and enthusiasm
have meant so much

SILHOUETTE BOOKS
300 East 42nd St.,
New York, N. Y. 10017

ISBN 0-373-82218-9

CHANCE AT A LIFETIME

Copyright © 1993 by Anne Marie Rodgers

Visit Silhouette at www.eHarlequin.com

Printed in U.S.A.

About the Author

Anne Marie Winston is a Pennsylvania native and former educator. She began reading romances a long, *long* time ago, and considers getting paid to write them the perfect occupation for an irrepressible reader! She and her family share their rural home with a houseful of four-legged critters. Her hobbies include figure skating, theater and dance, working in her gardens, canine rescue and inhaling as much chocolate as humanly possible. She cooks when it is absolutely unavoidable and spends large quantities of time chauffeuring children to extracurricular activities.

Anne Marie's 1993 novel, *Carolina On My Mind*, received the Reviewer's Choice Award from *Romantic Times Magazine* for Best Silhouette Desire. She has topped the Waldenbooks series bestsellers list, and several of her titles are listed on Amazon.com's list of 75 all-time bestselling Silhoutte Desires.

Books by Anne Marie Winston

Silhouette Desire

Best Kept Secrets #742
Island Baby #770
Chance at a Lifetime #809
Unlikely Eden #827
Carolina on My Mind #845
Substitute Wife #863
Find Her, Keep Her #887
Rancher's Wife #936
Rancher's Baby #1031
Seducing the Proper Miss Miller #1155
The Baby Consultant #1191
Dedicated to Deirdre #1197
The Bride Means Business #1204
Lovers' Reunion #1226
The Pregnant Princess #1268
Seduction, Cowboy Style #1287

*Butler County Brides

Dear Reader,

What would you do if you woke up and looked into the mirror at your face *and it wasn't your face you saw?* I watched a movie once in which the heroine's brain was transplanted into another, "plainer" woman. In the movie, the woman's husband couldn't see past her changed appearance to the heart within. It offended my romantic sensibilities, so I did the only thing any reasonable writer of romance would do: I created a hero who would recognize and love his woman no matter what.

This book is for every woman who has ever worried about her weight, her wrinkles, her under- or oversized body parts, her hair...never mind. This book is for every woman! Enjoy.

Fondly,

Anne Marie Winston

Please address questions and book requests to:
Silhouette Reader Service
U.S.: 3010 Walden Ave., P.O. Box 1325, Buffalo, NY 14269
Canadian: P.O. Box 609, Fort Erie, Ont. L2A 5X3

Prologue

PAIN...knives of hot agony slicing her with each shallow breath...*my God, make it stop*...voices fraught with urgency somewhere above her head....

"Somebody help me over here. We've got to get pressure on the leg—we're going to lose her if she bleeds much more."

"We need a type—*stat!*"

"Her husband said she's A-positive. Call for all the units they've got—we'll need them if we're going to save her."

The pain began to recede. *Ah, blessed relief*... She wanted to thank whoever had made the pain go away, but she couldn't form the words.

"Look at this head wound, Doctor. Scalp and surrounding tissue totally destroyed, cranium badly damaged—one pupil responding minimally.

"Prepare yourselves for the worst, kids. I don't think we can save this one."

"Even if we do, she's going to require total care for the rest of her life. There's spinal-cord damage."

"Damn! She's so young. What the hell happened?" an authoritative voice said.

"Her husband said she darted in front of a truck to save their little girl—apparently she got away from them on a street corner." This voice was female, already sounding defeated.

Carrie could see the woman who spoke. She was wearing a surgical mask, but tears trickled down from the corners of her eyes to make darker tracks on the blue fabric of her gown.

Looking at the mess on the table, Carrie could see why. A fall of wavy dark hair spilled over the edge of the metal ledge; bright blood dripped from it in a steady puddle onto the white floor. This must be an emergency room. The people scurrying around—a triage team?

The body on the table was in bad shape, but the face was the worst. Whoever it had been was unrecognizable now under the mask of blood, but Carrie was fairly sure that when it was washed clean, she wouldn't want to see what was left.

Yuck. She hated blood and gore. Ben laughed at her, but she wouldn't even watch a thriller with him anymore if it was too graphic. So why was she watching this?

She reached for the small black box that turned off the television—

—and realized she was reaching into thin air.

"Dear God!" It was a scream, but not one of the people below her looked up.

Below her! How had she gotten up here? Fearfully confused, Carrie examined herself. She was whole, she was in one piece, but she appeared to be floating near the ceiling of the white room. The woman on the table...long dark hair... *No!* What had the girl said? She'd saved her little girl and had been hit by a truck?

Daughter. Jennie. Where's Jennie? As easily as the thought came to her, she was moving. Not walking, not expending one whit of energy that she could perceive, but moving. Before she knew what it was, she had passed through a wall. *Through a wall!*

The truth came to her.

Oh, God. Oh, GodohGodohGod, please don't let this happen to me. I can't die. I'm only twenty-six years old. Ben needs me. Our baby needs me. Help me. Please, help me.

Another cubicle much like the one she'd left appeared below her. A woman, blond, inert, lay on the table here, with another frantic team working on her.

Another wall. Another cubicle. A man's body here, as blond as the woman she'd passed. Even from up here, she could see the sad resignation on the faces of the people in the room as a white-coated doctor solemnly shook his head and stepped away from the table.

Another wall. She was conscious of a feeling of speed, of moving faster and faster toward some unknown destination. Chairs, a desk...the familiar waiting room of the hospital near their home in Towson, Maryland. *Ben! Here I am! Ben. I'm all right.* But that wasn't so, was it? Broad shoulders shaking, dark head bowed, her husband slumped in a chair with his hand over his eyes. *Don't cry, my love.* Her heart swelled with the depths of the love she carried in her heart for the man who'd been her first and only lover. She wanted to reach out, to cradle his head to her breast and take away his anguish, but she was speeding on, past her mother-in-law, Helen, standing stricken at the far end of the room with Jennie in her arms. Jennie's thumb was in her mouth, her tumbled dark curls sweated. She had been crying.

Oh, God, no. I can't leave a twenty-month-old baby. We waited so long. And she's all I'll ever have. Please don't take me.

As fast as the thoughts whipped through her consciousness, she was outside the hospital, passing right through the red bricks and the big old shade trees nearby. It had been a sunny afternoon when she'd started for the park with Ben and Jennie, but the sunshine gave way to clear, sparkling stars as she traveled—upward?—onward?—*where?*

The stars began to dim as the light increased. It reminded her of sunlight. It was so white and dazzling she felt as if she should cover her eyes. But strangely she wasn't bothered by the brilliance. She was moving steadily, and it came to her that she seemed to be in some sort of long hallway. Almost a tunnel, really, like she imagined the subway tunnel would look if she got off where there were no stations and looked around. The chief difference was the light. Farther on, there appeared to be an ever greater radiance, if that were possible. She thought she should be afraid, but there didn't seem to be anything here in this wonderful warmth that could harm her.

Ahead of her, another…presence…moved forward. Almost a shadow, a mere passing of less light through the brilliance awaiting, but she knew it was another…another one like her. But she couldn't go! Ben…he needed her.

He'd always wanted a big family. She'd felt so awful for not being able to give him that. He hadn't blamed her, but she knew he'd had a terrible time accepting the doctor's edict. Things had been strained between them for the last several months…but she loved him so. She couldn't leave without letting him know how very dear he was to her.

The brilliance beckoned, promising every perfect thing of which she'd ever dreamed. It was a powerful lure, but still she hesitated. Far away, in another time, another life, she could see the hopeless set of those shoulders. She couldn't leave Ben.

And Jennie. Her darling baby. A precious little miracle they'd thought they might never have. Jennie needed her, too. No little girl should have to grow up without her mommy.

As Carrie agonized, turned back toward her husband, her child, a sudden rush of—energy?—passed by and through her, moving onward in a concerted force that left her stunned. She sensed great purpose in its passing. As it proceeded on and on into the tunnel of light, the other shadowy presence she'd detected suddenly burst into a glowing being, almost as if it was celebrating. The energy that had passed her drew abreast of the glow, hesitated for the merest instant—

—and as she watched, the two beings merged, becoming one shining beacon of light. An intense feeling of joy rolled back over her as the glowing presence moved on again, picking up speed until it was roaring forward, leaving her suddenly bereft.

She looked backward again, wanting so badly to go back and tell Ben. And then she was moving, reversing the path she'd traveled, the more-than-miles of journey back, back, back to the hospital. This time she came down from above, straight into the room where the gruesomely disfigured body lay. *Her body.* The team around the table was worn, exhausted, but clearly not frantic anymore.

"I feel for the husband, but it's really for the best," said the young woman whose tears stained her gown.

No! You can't quit! I'm back—I need that body. Fix me! But even as she silently screamed the demand, she could see that there was no fixing the lifeless shell of Carrie Bradford that lay crumpled on the table. Unwilling to admit defeat, she tried frantically to fathom how she could pour herself back into that damaged container.

Just for a little while, she promised herself. *Only*

long enough to help Ben understand that it's only temporary, that I'll be waiting for him.

Frantically her gaze darted around the room and it was as if the walls didn't exists. In the next room, the blond woman lay. Carrie could see from the face of the people there that they'd lost their battle, too.

Another body... *Did she dare?*

She moved—flew, somehow—to the woman's cubicle. Casting around, she sensed no other presence, nothing that might object to her crazy idea. This body looked fine. It was undamaged except for a purplish bruise on the forehead.

It was a frightful thought—an utterly insane, nothing-to-lose brainstorm. She had to get back to Ben. If she couldn't use her old body, perhaps she could use this one. But how?

Try as she might, she couldn't seem to will herself into it. Of course, she didn't know how she'd gotten out of her own body in the first place. *Please, please, God, I'll do anything, just let me go back. I'm not ready to leave Ben yet.* If she'd been able, she'd have been sobbing.

Somewhere in her consciousness, the light, the warmth and radiance that had so entranced her, was calling. Perhaps she should go. A part of her wanted to...and yet...*Ben.*

Suddenly the light was there, with her, flooding the small white room with its overpowering glow. And there was something more. For the first time, she sensed a presence connecting with her. Only it wasn't really a presence as much as it was a being, because in it she could clearly envision two separate and yet combined forces.

If you can use mine, I don't mind.
Go ahead. We don't need them anymore.
Someday you'll understand—you and Ben.

Carrie's view of the little white cubicle suddenly expanded to include the next room over. The body of the blond man still lay on the table, but now the face had been covered with a sheet.

With crystal clarity, Carrie understood. These two…people?…had been joined by bonds of love that had transcended the fragile flesh of their physical selves. The man—he'd been the one ahead of her on her journey. And he'd been joined by the woman who'd loved him more than she'd cared to live without him.

The sensation of communion faded, and she realized the two—the one?—were gone. But in their place came another presence. This one offered no reason for its entry into her consciousness. But the room grew even brighter until she was made uncomfortable by the degree of intensity the light projected. She couldn't define the manner in which it bothered her, but she felt exposed, as if every corner of her mind, her heart and soul, were being inspected for flaws. It moved over her, through her, and she envisioned herself as a slide under the bright white light of a microscope, with every tiny detail of her contents out for all to see.

Then, just as she was ready to flee, to hide from the all-knowing inspection, a wave of…approval… enveloped her. *Had she been judged?* Even as she sought to form a question, the presence was fading. And as it faded, Carrie realized she was being drawn closer and closer to the body on the table.

One

"**M**arina? You're officially discharged. Are you ready to go home?"

Slowly she turned away from the window of the hospital room where she'd spent the past several days. It was still difficult to remember that her name was Marina Devereaux now.

"I'm ready." Her voice sounded husky, but Marina's sister, Jillian, didn't seem to notice, so she supposed it must be normal.

"Good." The smaller woman, as blond as her taller sibling, crossed the room to give Marina an impulsive hug. "I can't wait to get you out of here. Maybe once you're back in your own home, some of your memories will come back."

Marina returned the hug. She'd never known the

love of a sister before. Jillian had been an exceptionally good friend during the past four days and every
time she mentioned Marina's supposed loss of memory, Marina felt an instant of guilt, and even sorrow.
It gave her an odd pang to realize that the sister for
whom Jillian thought she was caring had passed beyond human concerns.

"Perhaps," she responded neutrally. She could
hardly explain that her memory was perfect, that
she'd never remember all the childhood delights Marina had apparently shared with Jillian, that she'd hit
upon amnesia as a way of disguising what would
surely be fodder for every tabloid in the country if
ever the press should find out. Her memories were
those of Carrie Bradford, a woman who'd been buried
yesterday, according to the newspaper. She could
never share those memories with anyone again.

Thirty minutes later, Jillian unlocked the door of
the condominium Marina and her husband, Ron Devereaux, had shared. As she stepped aside to usher her
sister in, Jillian said, "I hope this won't upset you
too much. If you remember anything, I hope it will
be how happy you and Ron were here. He loved you
so very much." Her voice broke and she paused to
regain control. "I'm so sorry that Ron didn't survive
the accident, but I'm glad you did."

Marina put her arm around her...her sister. "I'm
glad, too, Jill. Will it upset you too much to talk about
it? I'm still not sure what happened and the doctors
haven't told me much."

"Maybe they want you to remember by yourself." Jillian sounded doubtful.

"I don't think they hold much hope of that. Many victims of amnesia don't ever regain memory of the traumatic incident that precipitated their condition." True enough. That was practically a quote from one of the texts her doctor had lent her when she'd requested more information on memory loss.

Jillian didn't look convinced, but she acquiesced. "You and Ron were out on the boat."

"We owned a boat?"

"Yeah—the *Lady of My Dreams*. Ron bought it right after you met, when he found out how much you loved to sail. You were out on the bay—"

"The Chesapeake?"

"Uh-huh. A man in a speedboat hit you broadside. His boat was damaged but he kept going. The authorities are still hunting for him."

"What happened to us?"

Jillian sighed and dropped into a cream-striped lady's chair in the foyer. "Are you sure you want to go through all this?"

"I'm sorry if it hurts you. I just want to get a clear picture in my head, that's all."

"The doctor says Ron's neck was broken on impact, that he died instantly. You were both thrown into the water and the *Lady* broke apart. Some people in a nearby boat saw what happened and came to help. When they got there, you were clinging to a piece of the hull, holding on to Ron's body. They brought you both in, and an ambulance met you at the dock. At the hospital, they could see right away Ron was dead, but you were still breathing. You'd ingested a lot of water and you had cracked your head on something, but they thought you were going to survive.'' Jillian looked up, and Marina could see tears streaking through her perfect makeup. "But when I got to the hospital, they told me your heart had stopped, that they couldn't figure out why they'd lost you, except that you must have suffered a greater head injury than they'd first thought."

"And then?" It was a bare whisper.

"And then, while the doctor was preparing the death certificates and I was being asked about organ donations from you and Ron, since he had no other family, a nurse came screaming into the room and said you were breathing again. She looked about as spooked as any person I've ever seen in my life!" Jillian smiled a little as she carefully blotted her makeup. She paused then and glanced up. "You have no memory of any of that?"

"Not a one." That wasn't a lie, she assured herself, uncomfortable with the evasion. She *didn't* have Marina's memories. Urging Jillian to her feet, she put an arm through the shorter woman's and said, "Show me around the condo. Pretend I've never been here before."

"What a weird feeling—showing my sister through her own home!"

"I know." Marina smiled wryly. "It feels pretty odd to me, too."

Jillian stopped in the middle of a perfectly appointed living room. "I wonder if the store will seem as strange?"

"I don't know. I'm anxious to see it. Maybe tomorrow." Jillian had told her they were co-owners and operators of a popular children's book and toy store called Kids' Place. They'd started it from nothing a decade ago. How in the world was she going to manage this? She'd been a homemaker since she'd graduated from college, and a mother for the last two years. True, her degree was in early childhood education, but Ben had felt strongly about having her at home, and she'd loved him so much she hadn't objected. And besides, she'd never minded being home.

As Jillian continued the tour, Marina followed thoughtfully, making little comment until they came to the large master bedroom that Ron Devereaux and his wife had shared. In a beautifully wrought silver frame on the dresser was a picture, the first one she'd seen in the condo.

Picking it up, she studied it quietly. The couple in the picture looked carefree and happy, totally confident of themselves and their life together. The photograph had been taken on a boat—the *Lady* Jillian had told her about? Ron stood on the deck, bare chested, wearing black swim shorts. His blond hair was wind tossed and his wide smile revealed deep dimples and perfect teeth. He'd been a handsome man and looked to be in excellent physical shape.

One hand was fisted at his waist, the other surrounded Marina. She was smiling as widely as he, directly at the camera. Her eyes were wide and blue, her teeth as beautiful as her husband's, set in a generous mouth. When the picture was taken, her hair was a bit longer than she wore it now, and a fine blond strand whispered across her husband's throat. Her body, in a figure-hugging orange maillot, was long and lithe, with slender legs that seemed to go on for miles. Her waist was so small her husband's hand covered her navel where he clasped her against him.

She was a beautiful woman. She was...*me*. For the first time, the enormity of her situation came to the new Marina, as she thought of herself. She could never go back to being Carrie Bradford, wife and mother. She was Marina Devereaux now, store owner, alone save for her sister. All she wanted to do was get close enough to Ben and Jennie to be sure they were doing all right without her....

And then what? She had a lifetime to live. She felt certain the loan of this body wasn't a temporary gesture. How would she fill the thousands of empty hours in a year? In a decade?

Jennie went toddling through the autumn leaves littering the yard, giggling her high-pitched baby laugh as Major raced in a wild circle around her. Ben was ready to shout a command when the big dog stopped an inch away from knocking the child flat.

Ben couldn't prevent the fond smile that spread over his face as he headed toward his daughter. She was getting pretty steady on those chubby little legs. How he treasured these Saturdays! Precious snippets of a time that was passing too fast as Jennie grew and changed. "Time to come in, Jen," he called.

"Doan-wan-choo!"

Ben laughed. Everyone else's almost-two-year-olds were naming colors and family members. One of the first phrases *his* daughter had learned was, "Don't want to." His enjoyment faded as he thought of Carrie. She would have been thrilled with Jennie's rapidly developing speech. The accident that took her life had been over three months ago. God, he'd never envisioned celebrating Jennie's second birthday without Carrie. When would the sharp edge of grief begin to abate?

Maybe never, he thought dully. Or maybe in a million or so years, when the guilt subsided. If he'd been paying attention to Jennie that day, instead of brooding over the complications of her birth that had cost Carrie and him their dream of more children, his sweet, loving wife might not have dashed into the path of that truck. Perhaps God would forgive him, because he knew he'd never be able to wash his hands of the blood that had puddled around her as she lay in the street.

Major barked and ran to the far side of the enclosed yard, where he began leaping and jumping, growling in a guard-dog frenzy that would have frightened anyone who didn't know what a cupcake the animal really was.

"Major! Heel!" The dog ignored him.

Ben sighed. Carrie was the only one who'd had any control over the canine cretin. He'd kept Major inside all morning because the new neighbors were moving in and the dog went wild every time a truckload of belongings pulled in or out of the driveway next door.

Jennie was running past the shrubbery toward the fence, too, as fast as her little legs would move. Ben sighed again. He'd never have believed anyone who told him a two-year-old could be defiant. As he started toward the fence to collar both the dog and the child, a husky yet distinctly feminine voice ordered, "Major, *sit*."

To his astonishment, the dog's black-and-tan hindquarters settled on the ground at once. The silence was absolute.

A bit wary, Ben moved through the bushes and approached the vinyl-covered chain-link fence. Jennie stood on one side, babbling nonstop with one tiny hand clasping Major's fur.

On the other side, a woman knelt. She had the fingers of one hand extended through the holes in the fence. Major was licking them as if they were sugar-coated. The woman had been listening intently to Jennie, but she glanced up as he neared.

He'd intended to speak, but the words died unborn in his throat. The male inside him leapt to attention even as the widower disclaimed any interest. Her hair was blond—vibrant, sun-kissed and golden. Soft, wispy bangs feathered across her forehead. The rest of it was one length, a straight, swingy style that curved just beneath her chin. The skillful cut framed enormous gray-blue eyes that exactly matched her T-shirt. They were the dominant feature in her

small, heart-shaped face. Right now those eyes were
surveying him solemnly.

"Hello." She rose to stand on her side of the fence
and he saw that she was tall—maybe only a few
inches below his own six feet. "I'm Marina Devere-
eaux. I couldn't resist talking to your little girl. She's
precious." Even in repose, her wide mouth had curled
up at the corners. The smile that accompanied her
words radiated a warmth he hadn't felt in many days.
It poured over him, easing the lonely ache that strangled his heart.

"Thanks." To cover the way she'd unsettled him,
Ben said the first thing that came into his head.
"How'd you know my dog's name?"

Her eyes widened a fraction and the smile faltered.
"Y-you called him earlier. I heard you talking to
him."

Ben felt foolish. And irritated with himself. He
hadn't meant to come off sounding like a grouch. He
tried to smile as he extended his hand. "I'm Ben
Bradford and I apologize for my rudeness. The darn
dog never listens to me—I'm jealous of your instant
success."

Her smile came back, along with two deep dimples
that made perfect round depressions in the rosy flesh
of her cheeks. "I've always loved animals. Is he a
mutt?"

Ben nodded. Unobtrusively he wiped his palm
down the side of his jean-clad leg, trying to erase the
tingling sensation that still lingered where her small
hand had fit into his. "Part collie, part shepherd. Lo-

cal humane-society special.'' The words brought back a painful memory of Carrie dragging him down row after row of concrete walkways lined with wire cages. She'd fallen for the puppy with the huge feet the moment she'd seen him. "I kept him in earlier so he wouldn't bark his head off at the movers. Are you one of our new neighbors?"

"The one and only." She hesitated. "My husband was killed in a boating accident not long ago. I feel fortunate to have found this place. It's exactly what I'd hoped for when I decided I needed a change."

"Please accept my condolences." He knew all the lingo now.

She nodded, eyes on the ground.

He wanted to tell her he knew how awkward it felt when people said those well-used but sincere phrases. But he wasn't ready to talk about Carrie to a stranger, so he let the moment pass. "It's a nice neighborhood. We love it here."

"How old are you?" His new neighbor had crouched again and was talking to Jennie. When the child proudly held up one finger, she laughed. "I bet you'll have a birthday soon. And then you'll be two." She made a *V* with two slender fingers.

"November second," Ben said. "Then she'll be Daddy's big girl."

"Me two." Jennie giggled. She gave her father a sly grin that sparkled with mischief. "Dad-dee two."

Ben swooped her up and walked his fingers over her round little tummy. "Are you teasing Daddy? I'll gobble you up for lunch, Peanut."

Jennie squealed with joy. When he set her down, she took his hand and tugged. "Lunch, Dad-dee?"

Ben nodded and smiled at their new neighbor. "This child has a one-track mind. Mention food and she's starving. It was nice to meet you—good luck with the moving."

Marina smiled. "Thanks. I suspect I'll need it."

Ben swung his daughter up to sit on his broad shoulders. "Okay, Jen, lunch it is. I'll make you an omelet."

"I see? I he'p?"

The words floated back to Marina as the man and child, with the big dog bouncing along beside them, started for their house. Tears stung her eyes as the little group disappeared through the back door into the mudroom she knew lay just beyond. Angry with herself, she dashed the drops away.

You chose this, she reminded herself. *You didn't have to come back.* Squaring her shoulders, she slowly retraced her steps through the unfamiliar yard to the house she'd bought. Jill had thought she was crazy to give up the condo and move to this quiet suburban neighborhood near Towson, but she'd appeared to understand when Marina finally had told her she needed a fresh start.

Marina hadn't really intended to buy a house near Ben...she'd only wanted to be sure he was coping without her. But when she'd been driving through the neighborhood a month ago, hoping in vain to catch a glimpse of her husband and child, she'd noticed the For Sale sign on the Carsons' home. She'd had a few qualms about using Ron's life insurance payment to make the purchase, but after she thought about it, she knew Ron and the old Marina wouldn't care.

She hung her coat in her kitchen and made herself a cup of her favorite cinnamon-apple decaffeinated tea, but Ben and Jennie wouldn't leave her thoughts. She hadn't known they were in the yard when she went out to look at her new flower beds. It was almost time to plant fall bulbs if she wanted pretty blooms to chase away the snow next spring. Would Ben remember that this was the year the tulips in front of his house needed to be separated?

Probably not. Landscaping hadn't been one of Ben's priorities in the past, especially if it involved anything more innovative than trimming. The yard looked good—he'd been keeping up with the mowing. She'd nearly run when Major came barking through the bushes at her. Her response had been reflexive and he'd reacted to the tone of voice, even if it had a different vocal quality now. He'd acted as if he had known her—was it possible? Poor Major. She missed him, too. Then Jennie had crashed into view and Marina's heart had shrunk in upon itself in the painful effort not to grab her child and cuddle her as she longed to do.

It was the first time in over three interminable months that she'd even seen Jennie. Although she rejoiced in every new milestone evident in her baby's speech and movement, it hurt to think of missing all those new developments and the ones to come. She'd just crouched down to talk to Jennie when Ben appeared.

She'd have to be very, very careful in the future not to let her familiarity with his family show. The thing with the dog had puzzled Ben. And his reaction had thrown her completely. For an instant of trembling time, she thought he *knew.*

He was thinner than he should be, but he still looked so good. His straight dark hair was cut in the style she remembered. It fell casually over his forehead from the side part, and the sunlight had highlighted the cleft in his square chin that she'd always loved. His top lip still curved in the well-defined bow that she'd traced with her finger, but it was rarely smiling as she remembered. Nor were the green eyes laughing as they'd always been.

Ben looked tired. But more than that, he looked unhappy. The only time the sadness in the depths of his gaze lifted was when he talked to Jennie.

In a way, she knew how he felt. She'd lost everything, even herself. Weekends were the worst—huge empty blocks of time that left her too many minutes to fill. The middle of the night was bad, too, when she wanted to snuggle up to Ben and found a cold pillow next to her. Or worse, when she thought she heard Jennie cry out. Sometimes she was on her feet, moving down the hall, before she remembered.

Her breath hitched unexpectedly. She set down her mug of tea with unceremonious haste as a wave of misery engulfed her. *Dear God, is this what the rest of my life will hold? Snatching glimpses of my hus-*

*band and daughter once every month or so if I'm
lucky?*

She was already working as many hours as she
could, filling her life with the store in a way that
amazed her sister. But she needed something more.
Something to keep her from running next door and
offering to scrub the floors of her former home if it
meant she could see Ben and Jennie again. Something
to fill the empty, restless nights when her body remembered that her husband slept just a few hundred
feet away. Something like a pet.

Not one to indulge in much self-pity, Marina considered the thought as she raised the hem of her shirt
and wiped her eyes. *Not a bad idea, Ca—Marina.* A
pet would be company and comfort in her home. Yes,
an animal to whom she could offer the well of now-
untapped love inside her might be just the thing.

"Go tree-tree *now!*" Jennie hopped up and down
in an agony of anticipation on Ben's front porch.

"Okay, Peanut, it's time. Let's go." Ben shut the
door on Major, leaving the dog barking inside. No
way was the mutt going trick-or-treating with them.
He palmed the small video camera he'd been using.
Taking Jennie's hand, he helped her down the steps
and directed her along the sidewalk. When they got
to Marina Devereaux's, Ben paused for an instant.
But her porch lanterns were on, so she must be expecting kids. He opened the gate and ushered Jennie
inside, then closed it behind him.

"All right, Jen," he coached the little girl. "You

go up to the door and knock real hard. When Mrs. Devereaux comes, you say 'Trick or treat!'"

Jennie toddled up the walk and carefully mounted the single step, the tail of her lion costume dragging behind her, as Ben hung back to film the event. When she turned and looked at him doubtfully, he ran up and rang the doorbell, then leapt back a pace again.

The door opened almost immediately. Marina's face broke into a huge smile when she caught sight of the tiny lion on the stoop. Damn. She was even more beautiful than he'd remembered, in a pink sweat suit that clung to her curves.

"Oh, dear," she said, her eyes wide as she opened the door. "Is this a ferocious lion? I hope she won't eat me."

Jennie looked over her shoulder at Ben again, her little face uncertain inside the hooded costume.

"Go ahead, Peanut," he said. "Remember what to say?"

Marina crouched down to Jennie's level. "I have some special treats here for hungry lions tonight." She showed Jennie a bowl of goodies. "Do you know what we say at Halloween?"

Jennie grinned and leaned against Marina's knee. She flirted through her eyelashes but she didn't say a word.

"Come on, Jen," Ben called. "You remember what I told you to say?"

"Tree-tree!" Jennie shouted, suddenly recalling her line.

Marina's face lit up like someone had just given

her a precious gift. "What a smart cookie you are, Jennie!" She offered the candy bowl and let the tot select two pieces.

"I can hardly believe she's old enough to start trick-or-treating," Ben said as he continued to film the scene. "She's gotten so independent these days. Everything we do, she wants to try by herself."

"It must be hard for you to let go," Marina said.

Ben nodded, watching absently as Jennie carefully backed down the step, sat and began trying to tear the paper from the candy bar she'd chosen. "It's a bittersweet delight to watch her growing up. Part of me wants to keep her small and helpless forever. But I'm a little relieved that she's not clinging to me tonight." He hesitated, then decided that now was as good a time as any to test the way it felt to explain about Carrie. He turned off the video camera. "My wife was killed in a pedestrian accident in July. Jennie's too young to understand completely, but it's been hard. She saw her mother hit by a truck." He left the bald statement hanging, unable to get any more out. He couldn't look at Marina; he was afraid any hint of sympathy would be his undoing.

"Dad-dee! See doggy!"

Ben glanced around at Jennie's exclamation just as Marina moaned.

"Oh, *sugar!*" The pseudo-profanity carried a wealth of chagrin. A small white dog dashed through Ben's legs at the same moment and Marina bolted off the stoop in hot pursuit. Jennie squealed with delight.

Ben stood, rooted to the spot. Carrie had used that

very same exclamation when she was exasperated beyond belief. He watched as Marina cornered the shivering little dog in the front yard and slowly, carefully, picked it up. He wondered who had taught her to say that, and if she ever swore. Carrie had hated profanity with a passion. After Jennie was born, he had to have a good reason to say "Damn" in his own home.

His blond neighbor came back to the stoop with the dog cradled in both arms. "Sorry about that. I just got her. She was abused and she's afraid of me and everything else coming down the pike." Her gaze met Ben's. "I'm sorry about your wife. Life is crummy sometimes, isn't it?"

"Yeah." Ben needed to change the subject. Tonight was difficult enough to get through without thinking of Carrie. He put out a hand to the white dog. She shivered and whimpered in Marina's arms. "She's petrified, isn't she? What's her name?"

"I call her Lucky. Because she's lucky to have a second chance. Her previous owners locked her in a closet with no food or water when they were away. When they were home, they beat her every time she barked."

Ben was incensed and it came through in his tone. "That's terrible. People should be arrested for that kind of abuse. How did you find her?"

"I went to the humane society. There's a long-haired white cat inside, too. I'm kind of a sucker for animals." Marina shrugged sheepishly. "And I needed some company. This big place is awfully empty."

Her eyes were hollow. Ben could see the pain before she dropped her lashes, shielding her thoughts from him. He missed the warmth she usually radiated. "Why don't you stop over tomorrow and relieve me of some of Jennie's c-a-n-d-y? I don't want her to eat it all, so you'll be doing me a favor." As soon as he closed his mouth, he wondered why he'd just issued an attractive, single woman an invitation to his home. He wasn't in the market for a replacement for Carrie.

"Thank you, but I don't eat the stuff. Poison."

Again, Ben was struck with a feeling of déjà vu. *Carrie could have uttered those words.* "My wife felt exactly the same way," he said before he thought about it.

Marina's eyes shifted away from his. She glanced down at Jennie. Her face relaxed as a grin replaced the look of...anxiety, almost, that had spread over her features. "Apparently, your daughter doesn't." She turned toward her door with Lucky. "Wait, let me get my camera and a damp cloth before you make the rest of your visits."

Ben looked down at Jennie and burst out laughing. The toddler was sitting on the stoop, oblivious to the adults' conversation. She had chewed open one end of the paper covering the candy bar Marina had given her and was busy sucking on the chocolate mess protruding from it. Her face and hands were filthy. With her hair covered and two ears topping the lion's head, she made a hilarious sight.

Marina hurried back out the door as he stood regarding his daughter. She knelt on the sidewalk and snapped a shot of Jennie, then motioned to Ben. "C'mon, you, too. I'll give them to you after I have them developed. This should finish off the roll." After Ben sat beside Jennie and grinned for her camera, Marina set it aside and gently cleaned Jennie's face and hands before dropping a quick kiss on her fabric-covered head. "Have fun, dollbaby."

She flashed another one of those warm smiles at Ben. "Thanks for bringing her over. You made my evening."

Ben nodded, feeling suddenly awkward. "We'll see you again." He hustled Jennie down the walk and on to the next house on the block. He wasn't attracted to her. He'd loved Carrie—he still did. So why did he want to turn around and spend the rest of the evening in her soothing company?

Two

Marina let Friday pass without taking Ben up on his invitation. She wanted to, badly, but she'd seen the panic on his face the minute he'd made the impulsive gesture. He was still grieving for his wife.

On Saturday she picked up the photographs she'd taken earlier in the week. She'd had the developer make double prints of the last few negatives—she couldn't resist the opportunity to keep a visual memory of her very own. These might be the only pictures she'd ever have of Ben and Jennie. The rest of the shots were of her shop, her sister, her new home and her new pets.

As she knocked on Ben's door after her solitary evening meal, she told herself she wouldn't stay. She'd only come to deliver the pictures.

"Hello." Ben looked startled when he opened the door. He was wearing a lightweight cream sweater she'd gotten him for Christmas two years ago. Underneath, his broad shoulders looked a mile wide. His hair was disheveled and his cheeks were rosy; she wondered what he'd been doing.

"Hi! I got my pictures developed and I have the ones of you and Jennie. They're really great and I knew you'd want to have them." *Stop babbling, Marina.*

"Thanks." He smiled and stepped back. "Would you like to come in? Jennie and I were right in the middle of a bout of wrestling. You can referee."

She relaxed, returning the smile as she let him take her coat and hang it in the hall closet. "You may be sorry. My sister tells me I was a mean wrestler in my youth." As soon as the words were out of her mouth, she held her breath. *Sugar!* She'd always spoken before she thought—now it was a liability she couldn't afford. The last thing she wanted was to have to explain her amnesia to Ben. He was too quick not to notice the odd way she had phrased the information about her past.

Thankfully, he made no comment on her peculiar words. They turned the corner into the family room. Jennie was sitting on the couch with her shirt pulled up, a carelessly swaddled doll pressed to her chest. She smiled at Marina, but kept humming something under her breath to the doll.

Marina smiled back, then glanced at Ben with

raised eyebrows. "She takes this mothering business seriously, I see."

Ben grimaced. "You don't know the half of it." He turned his back to Jennie and whispered, "She's breast-feeding her baby."

Marina was astounded. "She's *what?*" A bubble of laughter rose and she unnecessarily tried to turn it into a cough. "Where in the world did she learn that?"

Ben was laughing, too. At her words, the light in his eyes dimmed somewhat. "I've been showing her pictures of her mother and there were some of Carrie nursing her. Then we saw a mother at the playground nursing her baby, and the next thing I knew, Jennie was trying it." He ran a distracted hand through his hair and it fell in a perfect slant across his forehead. "Heaven only knows what I'll be dealing with when she's a teenager. The mere thought gives me nightmares."

"In this day and age, I can see why."

Ben smiled, but now there was no joy in it. "Would you like a drink? We have apple juice, cranberry juice, milk, iced tea and water."

This time she wasn't about to fall prey to her own idiocy. If she named the brand of tea she drank, he'd think something was askew for sure. "Thanks. Some fruit juice would be fine."

Ben went into the kitchen and she walked across the carpet toward Jennie. The room looked much as it always had, with its forest-green-and-gold striped furniture and heavy wooden tables. Her favorite hammered brass bowl filled with potpourri was still displayed in a spot Jennie couldn't reach. Bookshelves flanking a fieldstone fireplace held a variety of Jennie's toys on the lower shelves. Marina didn't recognize a few of them.

"Are you the mommy?" She settled on the sofa beside Jennie.

The little girl nodded vigorously. "Yeth. My baybee d'ink mi'k fwom Mom-mee."

Marina was astonished. Quickly she counted. *Seven words in a row!* A wave of parental pride swamped her. Seven-word sentences before the age of two! "Your baby drinks milk from Mommy?"

"Uh-*huh.* Bay-bee like mi'k."

"Do you like milk, too?" She wanted to keep Jen talking.

To Marina's surprise, Jennie shook her head. "Jennie not d'ink mi'k. Mom-mee go 'way." The child was still tuned in to her breast-feeding role.

The lump that sprang into Marina's throat refused to leave, so she spoke around it. "Your mommy still loves you, Jennie, even if you can't see her anymore. She loves you very, very much and she'll always be in your heart." She knew her voice was too intense when she glanced up and saw Ben standing there with the drinks, and she attempted to lighten it. "She's going to be a great mother someday."

Ben stared into his drink for a moment, unsmiling. "Who says she'll want to be a mother? Jennie's going to grow up knowing there are no guarantees in life. No toddler should have to learn that life doesn't last forever. Who knows how Carrie's...passing...will color her perceptions of happily ever after?"

The words were raw with grief. Marina reacted instinctively, longing to tell him how wrong he was. *Life does last forever*. Half rising, she held out a hand to—

"Dad-dee?" Jennie's little voice held a tremor.

They both stopped and turned toward the little girl.

"Me want Mom-mee." One grubby thumb sneaked into her mouth.

Ben swiftly scooped her up. Holding her against his shoulder, he rubbed her small back. His eyes were closed and Marina could see the pain in his face. "I know, Peanut, I know. Why don't we get ready for bed so you can see Mommy in your dreams?"

Turning to Marina, he said, "I need to get her to bed. She does this most when she's tired."

Marina stood immediately, stifling the urge to shed tears. "That's all right. I should go anyway."

"No." Ben shook his head. "You haven't shown me the pictures yet." He gestured toward the entertainment center that dominated one wall. "Find some music you like. I'll be back in a few minutes."

She blew Jennie a kiss as Ben carried the tot from the room. Drawing the photographs from her pocket, she placed them on the coffee table. Then she turned toward the sound system. She didn't need to look through the numerous offerings to know what she wanted. One of her favorite albums was within easy reach. Apparently Ben hadn't used this much. She'd swear the compact disc was still in the same place she'd placed it last.

As the strains of closely harmonizing brass and acoustic guitar filled the air, she wandered idly around the room. When the vocals came in, she sang softly along. It was still hard to believe she could sing now. Carrie had loved music, but she couldn't carry a melody that anyone could recognize, much less attempt harmony. Marina's husky alto was a delightful surprise. These days, the notes she heard in her head came out of her mouth when she attempted to sing.

As she rose from the floor, where she'd been looking at a new dollhouse someone had gotten Jennie, she came face-to-face with...*herself.*

Ben had placed the picture on a shelf at eye level. She recognized the shot immediately, although it hadn't been blown up and framed last time she saw it. It was a close-up candid photo that he'd taken last summer...just weeks before... Before. Carrie was kneeling in the flower bed and the picture showed only her head and shoulders amid a sea of blooms. She'd been laughing at something outrageous Ben had said and her eyes were lit with merriment. Her curly dark hair was pulled back with combs, a style Ben had loved, and the snub nose that Jennie had gotten was sunburned.

Desolation. Looking at the picture, Marina knew an inconsolable sense of loss. The familiar features made her heart ache. For the first time, she truly understood that she was mourning, too. Not just her loss of life-style, but her very self. Until now, she hadn't even had access to a picture of her old self. God alone knew what she'd give to look in a mirror and see that face again. Tears blurred her vision as she picked the photograph up and traced the features with a trembling finger. A drop of salty moisture plunked onto the glass and she hastily wiped it away.

When two hands came down on her shoulders, she nearly screamed. She turned around so fast she bumped Ben in the middle with the picture frame. "I'm sorry...I was just—"

"It's okay." His hands tightened and massaged for an instant. "I'm getting used to seeing Carrie's face. When I first put that picture out, it was tough to glance up and see her there, but I needed to do it for Jennie. And maybe for myself, too." His voice caught. He took the picture from her limp fingers and replaced it on the shelf.

"It's just so hard...." Marina shook her head helplessly as more tears spilled. She hated deceiving Ben. But she could never explain why she was really crying.

"I know." His voice was thick, too.

Unable to stop herself, Marina put a hand to his face. It slipped along his rough-whiskered jaw and into his thick, straight hair. *This is why I couldn't leave. He needs me.* She wrapped her arms around his strong shoulders as they began to shake. His big hands came up to her back in a convulsive grip that spoke volumes.

How long did they stand there, exchanging the comfort of human caring? Marina didn't know, but as her sobs abated, she became aware of how closely she was pressed against Ben's tall, hard body, of how intimate this embrace suddenly seemed. Despite her body's urging to stay right here where she belonged, alarm bells rang in her mind. He was quiet against her as she backed away. Her legs brushed his. Her breasts and belly felt unpleasantly cool with each step she took away from him.

"Uh, I'd better be getting home." She couldn't meet his gaze until he placed a finger beneath her chin and tipped her face up.

"Thanks for letting me cry on your shoulder."

"It was a mutual thing, remember?"

"Yeah." His regard was intense. "I guess only someone else who's grieving can understand the feelings."

"I guess." Her gaze slid away. This wasn't a topic with which she was comfortable. She felt almost as if she was lying—and that wasn't acceptable to her. She had vivid memories of being…evaluated. The rest of her life had to be lived with as much honesty and kindness and sensitivity as was humanly possible. She moved completely away then, severing the contact and heading for his front door. "The pictures are on your coffee table."

"Thanks. I'm having a little birthday dinner for Jennie on Tuesday evening. Would you like to join us?" Once again, he looked almost surprised at himself for inviting her over.

She deliberated. She really shouldn't. Being involved with his family was dangerous. But she doubted any woman in the world possessed enough willpower to deny herself a chance to be near her husband and child again. "You're just asking me so I'll take pictures," she said with a tentative smile.

Ben snapped his fingers, and she was lost when his familiar roguish grin appeared. "You saw through me. Is that a yes?"

She berated herself the whole way down his front walk and up her own. *You weak-willed wimp. You're going to have a heck of a time keeping yourself out of their hair on a daily basis. This is getting too important, Marina.*

She forced herself to face the fact that this invitation didn't mean she'd see them any more frequently. She couldn't get too chummy. Ben might think she was crazy and then she'd never see either one of them again. A horrifying thought struck her. What if Ben moved? Then they'd be out of her life for good. Even worse, what if he remarried?

It wasn't inconceivable, she knew. Ben was a charmer. Women would be falling all over themselves to get his attention after they knew he was...free. She had no doubt that he'd loved her—or Carrie, anyway—but he was only thirty-two. A man alone raising a small daughter. A man who'd made love to his wife nearly every night of their married lives. A man for whom a large family would be the crowning achievement of his life.

She winced, remembering the distance between them on that last walk to the park. She hadn't known what to say to him, how to console him. And she'd been stifling her own anger, her own grief at the loss of her dreams. Maybe she'd been a little fearful, too. Fearful that Ben wouldn't love her anymore if she couldn't produce the family he'd always wanted.

No, she couldn't imagine Ben staying single, however much he might be grieving now.

Late Tuesday afternoon, Marina whistled as she inventoried a supply of little metal animals that wound up with a key. The store was quiet and Jillian had suggested that they take the opportunity to check their stock for last-minute Christmas orders. Marina counted steadily, but her mind wasn't on the figures. Jennie's party was tonight. Tonight she'd see Ben and Jennie again.

"Do we need to order more of those before Christmas?" Jillian's voice intruded into her euphoria. "They've been selling since the day I put them out."

"I think we'd better," Marina replied.

Jillian made a note on the sheet in front of her. "Okay, that should do it. I'll get this out tomorrow." She checked her watch. "Time to close. Want to go out for dinner? I'm at loose ends tonight."

"What, no date?" Marina feigned shock. She could count on one hand the number of times Jillian had had a free evening since she'd…met her.

"No date, smarty. I thought you might appreciate an evening of your sister's undivided attention, so I left a night free."

Marina grinned. "You're too kind. But actually, I have plans. Could we make it another night?"

"Sure." Jillian looked surprised—and maybe a bit concerned. "Dare I ask what kind of plans?"

"Nothing much. My neighbor is having a birthday party for his little girl. She's two today."

"Your *male* neighbor?" Jillian's eyebrows rose when Marina nodded. "Does this neighbor have a wife?"

"His wife was killed in an accident last summer." Marina concentrated on the wooden tops she'd been counting.

"Wow...that's coincidental. How'd you meet him?"

"Over the fence one day." It was difficult to sound nonchalant.

"What's he look like?"

"I suppose you could call him tall, dark and handsome, if you wanted to be trite."

Jill shook her head. "You must have some internal mechanism the rest of us are lacking. Ever since we've been old enough to notice boys, you've been snagging the gorgeous ones. Trust you to wander home with a specimen that exudes sex appeal like sweat."

"From what I've observed, you snag your share, too," Marina said. "Besides, all I did was talk to him. He's still grieving—he's not interested in a relationship any more than I am right now." She crossed her fingers, even though it wasn't strictly a lie.

Her sister looked sympathetic. "Perhaps it will help you both if you have someone to talk to who understands." She paused. "Have you told him about Ron?"

"Just the facts you gave me."

"You haven't remembered anything else?" Jillian held up a hand before Marina could speak. "I'm sorry. I promised myself I wouldn't bug you about it. It's just so darn hard to believe that your mind is like a clean slate. I keep wanting to say 'Remember this, remember that?' and then I realize you don't."

Marina didn't miss the edge of desperation. She stood and hugged her sister fiercely. "I know how tough this is for you, Jill. If I could remember for you, I would." *But I can't. Because I'm not the Marina you grew up with, the sister you loved.*

Sometimes she was tempted—so tempted—to unburden herself, to share the confusion and pain that she lived with every day. But she couldn't do that to Jillian. Jill would be devastated if she ever understood that her sister was gone. Marina had grown to love Jill, to delight in the easy relationship Carrie never had had with a beloved sister. Jillian had been her rock as she'd struggled to find a focus in those first empty days. She wouldn't—couldn't—do anything to cause her pain.

"It's probably better this way." Jillian squared her shoulders. "I'm almost glad you're not grieving for Ron. When you two met, it was as if—as if neither of you could see anyone else. I've never seen a couple so in love. You were married ten days after you met, and five years later you were still as much in love as you were the day you exchanged vows. I honestly don't know how you'd have handled losing him.''

''Perhaps I wouldn't have.'' Marina's voice was sober. In her mind's eye, she saw again the joyous explosion of light as the two...presences met and melded. Yes, she could believe Ron and Marina had been in love. She thought of Ben. Did he and she— had he and she shared a feeling that powerful? She still loved him with every fiber of her being...the way Marina had cared for Ron?

She locked her house behind her in the late afternoon and headed purposefully down her walk and up to Ben's front door. On her arm was a basket with three gaily wrapped packages spilling out. It had been wonderful selecting a birthday gift for her daughter, but sobering to know she should only take one or two. It was five o'clock. If her routine hadn't changed, Jennie would have had a nap and be bright eyed again.

She wasn't disappointed. The minute Ben opened the door, Jennie danced out. Ben was right behind her. In navy pants and white shirt with the top button undone, he looked so handsome that Marina had to search for a small smile that did nothing to indicate the way her heart raced.

''Hi.''

She struggled to cover her breathlessness. ''Hi.'' Was the warmth in his eyes for her?

''Me party! M'rina have p'esents for me?''

Marina laughed as she squatted down to Jennie's

level. "What do I have in this basket? Is it someone's birthday today?"

Jennie squealed and giggled. "Uh-huh."

"Oh, I know. I bet it's Daddy's birthday. Should we give him these presents?" Marina made as if to hand the basket to Ben.

"Not Dad-dee! Jen-nie's birfday." The tot anxiously poked a stubby finger into her own chest.

"Jennie's birthday! Are you sure?"

"Uh-*huh!*"

"Well, then, these presents must be for you."

Ben chuckled as Jennie fingered the beribboned packages hopefully. "Wait a minute, Peanut. We aren't going to open them yet, remember? Let's take Marina in and introduce her to Gramma." He closed the door behind them as Jennie took Marina's hand and tugged her into the family room.

"Gramma? See me's p'esents?" The child dropped Marina's hand and ran across the room to an older woman, pointing at the basket Ben was carrying.

The woman stood. She'd once been nearly as tall as Marina herself. Her hair was white, short and neatly styled, and her inexpensive sweater and slacks were perfectly pressed. Her eyes were the same piercing hazel-green as her son's. Right now they were looking at Marina with a distinct challenge in their depths.

"Mother," Ben said, "this is our new neighbor, Marina Devereaux. Marina, my mother, Helen."

Marina exchanged a hand. "It's nice to meet you, Mrs. Bradford." She'd learned the hard way not to let Helen intimidate her. She'd never make that mistake again.

"And you, also," Helen returned. Her handshake was firm and decisive, but brief. As soon as she released Marina's hand, she turned toward Jennie. "Here, sweetheart, let me help you put the presents on the table until after we eat."

As Jennie and her grandmother turned away, Ben said, "We're almost ready to eat. It'll just be a few minutes."

"Can I help?" Marina followed him toward the kitchen, wanting to give Helen some space. Helen had been reserved and distant with Carrie for a long time, until she'd been convinced that Carrie loved her only son more than anything in the world. When she'd finally accepted her, it had been total. Knowing Helen as well as she did, Marina was sure it wouldn't be easy for her mother-in-law to accept any woman in Ben's life so soon after Carrie's death.

But she wasn't in Ben's life. Was she?

"You could put those on the table in the dining room." Ben indicated a stack of dishes and cutlery on the counter. "I let Jennie choose the menu tonight, since it's her special day, so I'm afraid we're stuck with spaghetti."

"I love spaghetti." As Ben turned toward the pot on the stove, Marina picked up the plates. She fought to keep her shock from showing in her eyes. *My kitchen!*

She loved to cook, had always kept her kitchen immaculate. Ben apparently had other things on his

mind. It wasn't exactly dirty, she realized. Just...
cluttered. On the long counter where she'd done most
of her cooking, a wide variety of toys that Jennie
could only play with under supervision was haphaz-
ardly piled. She shuddered to think what the inside of
the walk-in pantry must look like. The battery-
operated clock on the wall had stopped at seven
minutes past two. On the shelves flanking the window
above the sink, sad-looking pots in gay containers
boasted dead leaves instead of African violets bursting with blossoms. A philodendron hanging from a
hook in the dining alcove had fared slightly better,
but its leaves were a sickly yellow. The built-in desk
in the far corner was concealed beneath a dangerously
high stack of books and papers, magazines, catalogs
and junk mail.

She held her breath as she stepped slowly into the
dining room, but here, like the family room, things
appeared to have been largely undisturbed. She
quickly set the table, leaving Jennie's little dish set to
one side.

As Ben came in with a steaming bowl of spaghetti
sauce, she asked, ''Where's Jennie's high chair? I'll
set her things on her tray.''

''She doesn't use a high chair.'' Ben pointed back
to the kitchen table. ''Her booster seat is in there.''

Marina closed her eyes briefly as she went to get
the small chair. *She'd missed so much!* As she
brushed the crumbs off the seat, she banished the
lump in her throat. This was better than the alterna-
tive. At least she was here, sharing Jennie's birthday.

The meal was festive as the three adults let Jennie have the spotlight. After they'd finished eating, Ben took Jennie off for a diaper change before her party began.

Marina automatically began to clear the table.

"You don't have to do that," Helen said. "You're a guest."

The implication was clear. Marina picked up another plate. "I don't mind. Living alone, I hardly have to worry about dishes."

"You're not married? I would think that house would be a bit much for a single woman."

Marina knew from experience that Helen's overprotectiveness was a habit rather than a deliberate attempt to annoy. Ben's father had died when he was a small child and Helen had had to work throughout his formative years to support them. Aloud, she said, "My husband was killed a few months ago and I just couldn't stay in our home. I love yard work—it's soothing for me, so the place was irresistible."

Helen looked shocked. "Oh, my dear, I am so sorry. You know Ben lost his wife in July?"

"Thank you." Marina nodded as they returned to the dining room for another load. "He's spoken of her."

Helen's eyes glimmered with tears. "Carrie was…perfect for Ben. I loved her like a daughter. This has been devastating." She set down a load of glasses on the counter and went back to the dining room again.

Marina pulled a plastic dishpan from beneath the

sink and proceeded to fill it with sudsy water. As it filled, she opened the dishwasher and began to load it. When Helen came into the kitchen again, she gasped. "You don't have to do that. I'll clean this up after Jennie opens her presents."

"It will only take a moment. It was kind of you all to include me and this is the least I can do."

"Well...thank you." Helen gestured toward the garage. "I'll get the ice-cream cake out of the freezer so it can thaw while we play a few games."

She'd barely disappeared through the door when Marina plunged into the dishes. As she washed the few items that couldn't go into the dishwasher, she also wiped down counters and cleaned off dusty shelves. Several of the violets still had some green leaves trying to sprout in their centers, so she watered them. Then she carried water to the philodendron.

Just as she finished giving the plant a drink, Ben came back into the kitchen carrying Jennie. "What are you doing?" He didn't sound pleased.

"I offered to wash the dishes so Helen could get out the c-a-k-e, and I noticed that your plants needed water." She set down the small pitcher she'd been using, then crossed her arms and rubbed her palms over the opposite elbows.

Ben was staring at the movement of her hands. "They were really Carrie's plants. I'm no good with them."

She smiled, trying to ease the indefinable tension, and dangled the little pitcher in the air. "You might be surprised at how well they do with a little watering.''

Ben's wide shoulders rose and fell. "I forget. Why don't you take them with you when you go? I don't really want them.''

"Oh, no," she said. "African violets are very particular about their sunlight. This east-facing window should give them perfect exposure. How about if I try to remind you to water them? I think a few of them will come back if you do.''

"Whatever.'' Ben shrugged again. He was still examining her with an intense regard that made her want to squirm. "Please don't take this the wrong way," he said at last, "but you have the strangest resemblance to my wife.''

"But I don't—''

"You don't look a thing like her, I know, but some of the things you do are so like her, it's eerie.''

Marina crossed her arms. "Coinciden—''

"There!" He pointed at her. "Carrie used to do that all the time when we argued. I could always tell when she was feeling defensive.'' His green eyes narrowed. "Am I making you nervous, Marina?''

"Of course not.'' She dropped her arms and straightened her back. She'd never even thought of this. Half the things she did were instinctive, without conscious thought. She'd be hard-pressed to change herself in that way, even if she wanted to. "I'm sorry if things I do remind you of your wife. It's not deliberate.''

Ben nodded, but his gaze never left hers. "How could it be, when you never even met Carrie?''

Three

"**H**ap-py Birth-day to you!"

Jennie beamed as the song ended and her cake, complete with three lit candles, was set in front of her.

"And one for good luck," Marina said when Jennie began to blow out the tiny flames.

That was one way Marina certainly didn't remind him of Carrie, Ben mused as he zoomed in on Jennie's face with the video camera. Marina had a pretty, musical voice. Even her speaking voice was melodious. Carrie had cheerfully acknowledged that she couldn't carry a tune in a bucket.

But still...it was damned unsettling. A certain way she tilted her head when she was amused, the crossing of the arms when he made her uptight, even the way she'd caught her tongue between her teeth as she'd watered the plants before she'd seen him come in.

Weird. And even worse, arousing as hell. The familiarity of her movements seduced him into feeling more at ease with her than he had with any other woman in his life, except Carrie.

But he'd spoken the truth when he'd said she looked nothing like Carrie. His wife had been short and well-rounded, tending to plumpness if she wasn't careful about her diet. Marina was all sleek angles and slim curves. Her breasts wouldn't fill his hands the way Carrie's had, but her long, well-muscled legs were a man's dream. He could imagine them wrapped around his waist, tightening to press him deeper—

Damn! What was the matter with him? He'd loved his wife. He wasn't looking for a replacement. Besides, she certainly didn't seem to be on the make. Despite his body's fascination with his neighbor's cover-girl beauty, he'd swear she was completely unaware of her looks. She didn't behave like a woman accustomed to men's adulation. She was sweet and friendly, she liked his daughter...and she was sexy as all hell.

Did she have any inkling of how close he'd come to kissing her the other night? The embrace they'd shared had begun as a comforting closeness, a need to give solace to another grieving soul. He'd been incredibly touched that she'd shed tears for Carrie. It had been a time of mutual comfort, of sharing the horror and loss that only someone whose heart-mate had been killed could understand. But beneath the warmth and tender caring they'd shared, there'd been a thread of awareness. Her slim, tall figure pressed against him lit fires that had been smoldering since Carrie's death. He was fairly certain the attraction hadn't all been on his part. He'd heard the intake of a shallow gasp, the increased rhythm of her breathing. If he'd pressed a finger to her pulse point, he knew it would have been racing to match his.

Sex. That's all it was. Man wasn't designed to lead a celibate life. Men and women were made to excite each other in the same way that countless other animals did. Procreation demanded it. The sole difference between man and other animals was that a man could choose not to act on his impulses.

His impulse had been born of a noble urge. But somewhere along the way, his body had forgotten about comforting and had focused on copulation. He'd been as ready as Major had been last week when the collie across the street had gone into heat. Hell, he still was. He'd read about pheromones, invisible scents that animals exude. Marina's pheromones were calling him loud and clear.

Was she as hungry as he for a simple kiss? For the warmth of another body? For the momentary satiation and utter relaxation that followed great sex? They were both lonely. Maybe she was interesting in a no-strings, no-emotions affair that would offer solace, of at least one kind, to them both.

In your wildest dreams, Bradford. He was immediately ashamed that he'd even entertained the notion. Jennie finished her cake as he pushed away his erotic thoughts. He laid down the video camera and grabbed the still camera for a quick shot of her wide eyes as Helen and Marina set piles of presents on the table.

"Here, sweetie, this one is from Gramma." Helen placed the first of many packages in front of Jennie. It was a tedious process, trying to get Jennie to open all the gifts. When one toy appeared, she wanted to play with it. Talking her into setting it aside for yet another wrapped present was a challenge for a saint. Looking at the stacks of gifts, he guessed maybe he'd overdone it a little.

Marina handled it all with aplomb. She cajoled Jennie with finesse, seeming to know just how far she could press before the little girl balked. Ben would swear she had children of her own.

Maybe she did once. The thought made his blood run cold. She'd said only that she'd lost her husband. He'd never considered that perhaps she'd had children, as well. Would she talk about it if she'd lost a child? Losing Carrie had been horrible, but what if Jennie had been struck down by that truck, too? He'd had nightmares about it dozens of times. If he'd lost Jennie, he knew he wouldn't be able to mention it in casual conversation.

"You seem to be very comfortable with children." Helen's chance comment paralleled his thoughts so closely he winced. Quickly he glanced at Marina to see how it had affected her.

But she was smiling. "I like children," was all she said.

"Do you have nieces or nephews?" His mother was nothing if not persistent.

"No." Marina wound up a hopping frog with its metal key and set it before Jennie. "But my sister and I own and operate a children's book and toy store called Kids' Place. We see lots of children of all ages come through the store. Some families frequent us so much that I've gotten to know their children's names and ages."

"Kids' Place...in Downington Plaza?"

When Maria nodded, Helen's eyebrows rose. "I've been there. You have quite a selection. I was very impressed with the quality of the toys you stock."

"Thank you. We believe in selling toys that will last, toys that stimulate a child's imagination. So many of the playthings on the shelves of so-called toy stores today are dependent on batteries and have only one function—" Marina gave a rueful smile. "Sorry. I tend to get on my soapbox about this issue. Actually my sister, Jillian, orders most of the toys. My specialty is children's literature."

Ben looked again at the gifts she'd brought Jennie as Marina and Helen continued to talk. The anthology of children's poetry was illustrated by a name even he recognized. He knew Jennie would love the flowing rhythms of the rhymes. A second package had contained a little white rabbit puppet the perfect size for a two-year-old. Right now, it took top honors as gift of the evening, since his daughter was clutching it to her chest. The third had held a house made of fabric that opened and closed with Velcro tabs. All the dolls and the furniture inside were made of stuffed fabric. It had been one of the toys with which Jennie hadn't wanted to part.

Marina clearly loved her work. He was aware of a nagging feeling of...disappointment? She was so like Carrie in her domestic capabilities that he'd just assumed she didn't work outside the home. He didn't want to think about why that bothered him.

Aloud, he said, "Sounds like it keeps you busy." She was watching him. He sensed resignation, almost as if she knew what he was thinking.

"I enjoy it. I've worked much longer hours recently...." She hesitated, then added, "There's only so much housework I can do, and I find it easier to be around other people."

He wanted to speak, but his mother beat him to it. Leaning across the table, she placed her hand over Marina's and said, "I admire you, dear. I know what it's like to lose a husband young. It takes a great deal of fortitude not to cave in to the loneliness."

Ben was amazed. When he'd first mentioned that he'd invited his female neighbor to Jennie's party, his mother had been almost hostile. He knew how much she'd loved Carrie and he guessed she was afraid he'd be so lost without her he'd marry the first body that came along.

Marina turned her hand palm up so that she was clasping Helen's hand. "It must have been much more difficult for you with a young child. I admire you and Ben. All I have to worry about are two pets." Withdrawing her hand, she glanced at her watch.

"And speaking of pets...I'd better be running. Lucky has lived up to her name, but I don't want to chance an accident."

Ben rose as she did. "Thanks for coming over. Jennie was excited about seeing you again."

"She's precious. Thank you for including me."

Helen broke into the goodbyes. "Looks like the birthday girl is on her last legs." She pointed toward the child, who was leafing through the book Marina had given her. Her eyelids drooped and her head rolled as she struggled to stay awake. "Why don't I put her down while you walk Marina home, Ben?"

Again he was mildly astonished. His mother was practically pushing him into his neighbor's arms! He really didn't want to walk Marina anywhere. She was too...disturbing. But he nodded, not knowing how to get out of it without seeming rude. "Thanks. I'll be back shortly."

Marina jingled her keys as Ben shut the back door behind them. She hesitated, then turned to face him. "This was a very nice evening. But you aren't obligated to walk me to my door. I don't want to put you out."

Was she a mind reader? Ben ran a finger around the collar of his white shirt. "It's no trouble." He realized it was true—walking with Marina would be a pleasure, despite his physical awareness of her. "Don't let my mother's less-than-subtle maneuvering make you nervous. She has a mind of her own and I'm never sure what she's going to say next."

"She's lovely. My mother passed away a number

of years ago and I still miss her." She was grateful to be able to utter the words without pausing. They were true. Marina's mother had died when she was sixteen, while Carrie's mother had died suddenly of a heart attack less than a year after her father's death.

"Mom's been a rock of strength since July. If she hadn't been able to help so much with Jennie, I don't know what I'd have done about baby-sitting."

"Does she come to your house?"

"No, I drop Jennie off at her place on my way to work in the morning. It works well because sometimes my schedule gets busy and I have to work odd hours. I'd have a tough time doing that with a hired sitter." He unlatched the gate that connected their backyards and waited until she'd passed through.

"If you ever get in a bind, I'd love to keep her."

He snorted. "She can be a handful."

"I'm serious. My schedule is flexible. She could go along to the store with me if I needed to pop in."

"Thanks. I'll keep it in mind." He couldn't think of a single good reason why he'd need to ask her to watch Jennie, though. His mother was almost fanatical about her recently acquired role.

"What type of work do you do?"

"I'm in investments...helping people use their money to make more money, tax shelters, that sort of thing. I sometimes have client obligations such as dinners and golf outings that run into the evening hours and I couldn't leave Jennie with just anyone. I guess I could find a job that had more predictable hours, but this is what I enjoy doing."

"It's important to do something that makes you happy. I never realized how much a fulfilling job could add to my life until..."

When her voice trailed away, Ben glanced at her. The sadness in her expression told him immediately what she was thinking. Almost automatically he reached for her hand. It was warm and smooth beneath his fingers, much smaller than his own. He was suddenly aware of how baby-soft her skin was.

Without planning it, without really meaning to, he pulled her to a halt beneath the big oak tree outside her back door. Her musky scent enveloped him as she swung around to face him with her back to the tree. The silence hummed with thoughts unspoken for a long moment. Her eyes were enormous; they searched his, slowly closing when his own gaze moved to her mouth. Could she possibly taste as good as her unspoken allure promised? His body urged him to find out.

He slipped his thumb up over her wrist to where he could feel her pulse. Its rapid thudding told him everything he'd been wondering about in the instant before she tore her hand away.

"Ben, I don't think... We could be neighbors for a long time and neither of us wants to have regrets—"

"What would you regret?" He recaptured her hand and its fluttering mate as he took a step closer.

Marina stepped backward and almost lost her balance on the brick border of the flower bed. When she toppled forward, their bodies collided and he nearly groaned aloud as he placed his hands at her waist and held her fast. *What are you doing Bradford? The woman's as recently bereaved as you are.* But even that mental caution wasn't enough to make him step away.

Marina was breathing hard, but he couldn't decipher her expression as she searched his face in the shadows. "You're a very attractive man. Too attractive for my peace of mind. One of the things I fear most...is hopping into bed with someone because I can't stand the loneliness. Sex is only a temporary solution."

"And you think that's why I'm—" The protest was automatic. No woman should be able to read a man so easily.

"Coming on to me." She nodded gently. "Yes. You loved your wife. What other reason could there be?"

He didn't want to think. Didn't want to admit that she might be right. What he wanted was to kiss her, to back her up against that tree and put his tongue in her mouth, to touch her all over until she was writhing in his arms and begging for more.

You loved your wife. It was true. He had loved Carrie. If she were alive, he'd never be seeking oblivion in any other woman's arms because—despite the hurt and misunderstanding that had affected their last few months together—she was the only woman he'd ever wanted. She was the thread that bound his world. Her death had torn a great hole in his life and he wasn't sure it could be mended. *Oh, God, for one more chance. I'd do anything to have her back.*

But Carrie was gone.

And it was Marina he held in his arms, Marina's slender hips pressed against his throbbing body, Marina's warm, sweet breath he felt on his flushed face. He was suddenly furious at her for pointing out his loss, for making him face the emptiness of his existence. For teasing him until he hurt with wanting her. Never mind that he couldn't recall a specific instance when he'd noticed her flirting with him.

"No other reason," he said, wanting to get to her like she'd gotten to him. "You're right—I did love my wife. And I'm not remotely interested in your mind, or your emotions. But my body's still alive, and when attractive women flaunt themselves in front of me, I damn well intend to take them up on their offers." Deliberately he rolled his hips against her in a crude movement, letting her feel the hard length of him, torturing himself in the hot cradle of her thighs. Then he thrust her away. "So stay away from me unless you want a sample of what you've been provoking."

The rain that fell intermittently all of the following week was the perfect foil for Marina's mood. On Saturday morning, more than a week after the disastrous evening with Ben, she dragged herself into the shop. Jillian was there ahead of her, as usual.

"Good morning," her sister sang out.

"'Morning." She hung her dripping umbrella and

raincoat on a hook in their tiny lounge and headed for the kitchenette. Jillian drank pots of strong, black coffee, but since the accident, when she'd learned Marina now preferred tea, she'd thoughtfully put on a pot of hot water each morning, as well.

Fortified with a mug of her favorite tea, she slipped the big pink apron she wore in the shop over her head and tied its sash behind her waist. Then she headed out front to open up the cash register.

Muffled sounds came from the storeroom at the back of the shop. They had received a new shipment of toys yesterday and she guessed Jill was already unpacking them.

"Look at these!" Jillian poked her head out of the storeroom. "Great stocking stuffers." In her hands, she held a variety of small, amusing items that would delight a child.

Marina managed a nod. The Christmas season was drawing closer and she found herself getting more and more depressed with every day that passed. This would be her first Christmas away from Jennie.... She'd been looking forward to it. *Before*. The thought of her baby leaving cookies out for Santa and hanging up her stocking—the one *she'd* cross-stitched before Jennie was born—sent her into a tailspin every time it entered her mind.

This would be her first Christmas without Ben since her senior year of high school, when he'd given her a tiny sweetheart ring. It was probably still tucked away in Carrie's jewelry box, waiting for Jennie to grow up so Ben could give her her mother's things.

Ben. Sweet Lord, she wished she could forget him. His unreasonable swing to rage had startled and frightened her the night of Jennie's birthday. She thought she'd understood how much he was hurting, but she hadn't really seen the depth of his anguish until then. And certainly for a man as physical as Ben, the grief was compounded by an element of sexual frustration that she hadn't thought about before.

Why had she persuaded herself that she could be a casual friend to Ben? Buying the house next to his was the stupidest move she'd made in her life—either of them. To be fair, she didn't think she'd been leading him on. But he was obviously attracted to her new body. Maybe she'd done things that she didn't realize. She wasn't an idiot—she knew that Marina was gorgeous in a take-a-second-glance way that quietly pretty, sloe-eyed Carrie hadn't been.

The ringing of the shop bell recalled her to her senses. She greeted the woman who came in, and left her to browse while she gift wrapped several items a customer had purchased yesterday. When the bell rang again, she glanced up—

—and sucked in a shocked breath of dismay when Ben's dark head appeared in the doorway.

He was wearing a navy rain slicker, but he hadn't pulled up the hood and his dark hair was plastered to his head. He'd been carrying Jennie and he paused to set her down, hunkering in front of her to help her remove the shocking pink raincoat she wore. Then he straightened and their gazes met across the length of the shop. He nodded without smiling and began to make his way in her direction.

Marina panicked. She didn't want to talk to him. If he was still angry, or even cool and distant, she was afraid she'd cry. Slipping out from behind the counter, she crossed to the storeroom. "We have some customers who need help," she announced to Jillian. "How about if I unpack for a while, since you're the toy expert?" Her voice came out breathless and too high.

Jill straightened and gave her a curious glance. "Okay. Are you all right?"

"I'm fine." Marina pressed a hand to her stomach. "Just a little indigestion. It should pass in a minute."

As her sister vanished out front, Marina sank down on a packing crate. *Great strategy. Hide from Ben every time you see him.* Resolutely she picked up the clipboard on which Jillian had been recording the items coming out of the box. She was just unwrapping the first one when Jill's head popped into the room.

"There's a man out here who'd like to speak to you, Marina. He has a little girl with him."

Marina feigned surprise. "Oh?" She set down the clipboard. "Is it one of our customers?"

Jillian looked amused. "No, it is not one of our customers. I suspect it's your tall, dark and handsome neighbor with the two-year-old. Remember him?"

"Oh. Yeah."

"Are you coming out, or shall I send him in?"

Marina shot to her feet. "No, no, I'll come out." The last thing she wanted was to be cooped up in that tiny room with Ben—and from the grin on her face, Jillian knew it. Marina stuck out her tongue at her sister's back as she followed her out of the storeroom.

Ben was standing near the small table they'd placed at one side of the store. He'd combed his hair and removed his jacket. On the table and some adjacent shelves was a variety of toys for children to use while their parents were in the shop, and Jennie was already making herself at home with a tiny tea set and a rag doll.

"Hello, Ben." Marina gave him her best professional smile. "Is this your first visit to Kids' Place? If there's something specific you want, perhaps we can help you find it." Jillian was hovering nearby, an expectant smile replacing her earlier smirk. Good manners forced Marina to wave a hand in her direction. "This is my sister, Jillian Kerr. Jill, this is my neighbor, Ben Bradford, and that's his daughter, Jennie."

Jill stuck out a hand and pumped Ben's enthusiastically. "It's nice to meet you, Ben. We hope you'll be a frequent visitor. Before you leave, be sure to fill out one of our customer cards for Jennie. We try to remember every child's birthday."

"Thanks." Ben looked bemused. "You two certainly do resemble each other."

"That's what people say." Jillian batted her lashes. "But once they get to know us, they realize that I'm really the great beauty in the family."

"And she's modest, too." Marina turned her sister

around and gave her a gentle shove. "Don't you have work to do?"

"Ta-ta." Jill waggled her fingers at Ben as she went toward the other customer. "It was *very* nice to meet you."

Ben was smiling when Marina dared to look at him again. "She's certainly not much like you once she opens her mouth."

"Thank you. I think. Jillian's twenty months younger than I am, but she did all the talking when we were small. People used to call me the quiet Kerr girl." She shut her mouth abruptly. What could he possibly want?

Ben was nodding. "You are quiet. You're friendly, but there's a bit more mystery to you, a reserve, that Jillian doesn't seem to have."

The words raised her internal defenses. *If he only knew!* She badly needed to get the conversation onto less personal ground. "Is there some way I can help you?"

"I'm not looking for anything in particular." Ben gave her a direct stare and she felt her heart skip into a faster rhythm. "I came to apologize for my behavior the other night."

"Oh, it's all ri—"

"No. It isn't all right." He slashed a hand through the air and she saw that he was still agitated, although he didn't appear to be angry with her. "I find you very attractive, Marina, and I chose to ignore your wishes and pursue that. What happened wasn't your fault and I'm sorry if I acted like a man on the make."

"I'm sorry, too, if I gave you mixed signals," she responded. "I've gone over it and over it, trying to figure out if I—"

"You didn't." Ben put his hands on her shoulders. "Listen to me. I was the one at fault." He dropped his hands and exhaled, and she mourned the loss of contact, impersonal as it had been.

She took a deep breath and smiled tentatively. "Is it okay if I accept your apology and we forget it?"

Ben nodded, tension evaporating almost visibly from his wide shoulders. "Sounds good to me. I've been flaying myself for two weeks. Friends?"

"Friends," she agreed. His eyes were a pure emerald shade today, shot through with tiny flecks of gold and black. She could have stood like a dolt and gazed into them all morning. The quiet bustle of the shop surrounded them, but neither noticed for a long, private moment. Then, with obvious effort, Ben tore his gaze from her face and looked around the shop. "This place looks interesting. Can I get the grand tour?"

She was still trying to calm her pulse, trying to tell herself *that look* meant nothing. "Sure. As you can see, it's not large, but we think we utilize the space pretty efficiently."

"You can say that again."

While Jennie continued to play within sight, Marina led Ben around Kids' Place. It was funny, she reflected, but she was as proud of the shop as if she'd really had a part in its inception and subsequent success. She'd certainly enjoyed learning everything she could in the last few months.

"This must take a lot of your energy." Ben spread his hands to encompass the room.

It was an innocent comment. So why did it put her on the defensive? "Any occupation to which one gives a lot of oneself takes energy. I love the shop. I was surprised at how much I enjoyed getting out of my house when I began to work."

"Some women enjoy staying home just as much."

"I don't doubt that. Being home, especially when one has children to nurture, is—must be—every bit as rewarding as a career in another field."

"Carrie stayed home, even before Jennie was born. She didn't need to work and I liked having her home. She seemed to be fulfilled by that." Ben's strong jaw had a stubborn set to it that she recognized.

Unobtrusively she circled the fingers of one hand around the opposite wrist to prevent herself from reaching out and stroking that aggressive line. "I'm sure she was," she said gently. "Given a choice that isn't dictated by financial necessity, I believe more women would like to be homemakers."

"Would you?"

She hesitated. "At one time, I would have said so. But I've never needed to work. This shop is strictly a labor of love. It always has been." That was true. According to Jillian, Marina had always wanted the shop. She'd certainly been married to a man who could keep her comfortably in style, but she hadn't been a woman content to travel the country club circles all day every day with nothing more pressing on her mind than what color to wear on her nails tomorrow.

Ben looked as if he would have spoken again, but the bell over the shop door jingled as another patron came in. Automatically Marina glanced at the heavyset man who'd entered. Her polite smile froze in place when he strode forward, opening massive arms as if to hug her. *Who was he?*

"Marina!" His face was wreathed in a grin. If he had a pipe clenched in his teeth, the fellow would resemble a black-haired version of Santa Claus. "How are you doing?" The smile turned to sorrow. "I surely was sorry about Ron. Missed you at the memorial service, but me and Milly have had you in our prayers."

"Thank you." It was the faintest of murmurs. Her mind raced through the names of people on whom Jillian had coached her. Jerry...the guy who had sold Ron the boat? She was pretty sure she had it right. To her everlasting relief, Jill appeared from behind her, sweeping forward to greet the exuberant stranger.

"Jerry!" Jillian clasped his elbow and forcefully turned the older man aside. "How good to see you!"

"You, too, babe," Jerry replied. "But it's even better to see Rina back in action."

Marina didn't catch Jill's murmured response as she practically dragged the fellow down the far aisle, but her tensed muscles began to relax. Meeting friends she was expected to know was always difficult, even when Jillian warned them about her amnesia. She was about to turn back to Ben when a sentence uttered in a booming masculine tone came floating from the far side of the shop.

"Amnesia? Ye gads, that's something you only hear about in books. Are you kidding me? Marina doesn't remember *anything?*"

Apprehensively she risked a glance at Ben. She could almost see the antennae rising as his eyes narrowed and he turned his gaze on her.

Four

The middle of November was a bit late to be putting in bulbs, but the weather had been unseasonably warm. This sunny Sunday was no exception. Marina knelt beside a shallow trough she'd dug in the soil around the patio at the back of her new house, methodically spacing red emperor tulip bulbs. Tamping the earth over the last one, she went back to the bags of gardening supplies she'd purchased and withdrew a sack of daffodil bulbs. Arranged in front of the large tulips, with another row of smaller orange tulips in front, it would make a beautiful bank of blooms in the spring.

Squinting at her watch, she realized that it would soon be lunchtime. Church was almost over, she remembered wistfully. She missed the church she and

Ben had attended after their marriage, the church where Jennie had been baptized, but she didn't dare start going back there. If Ben thought she was deliberately throwing herself in his path, who knew what he might do. This limited contact with her loved ones was torture, but it was certainly better than none at all.

"Hi, M'rina!"

Pleasure, sharp and sweet, whipped through her at the sound of the childish treble. Planting forgotten, Marina got to her feet and walked over to the gate that separated her yard from Ben's. "Hello, Jennie, how are you today?" After the brief conversation in the store a week ago, she hadn't caught a single glimpse of Ben or Jennie until this morning, when she'd seen them arriving home. They'd been dressed in good clothes. She assumed they'd gone to Sunday school, but they hadn't stayed for the worship service afterward.

Thinking of Ben reminded her again of the day he'd come to the store. She was sure he'd heard the comment about her loss of memory, but to her surprise, he hadn't mentioned it after that one speculative glance. Thank God. She wasn't sure she could look him straight in the eye and lie. The half-truths and evasions were difficult enough with Jillian.

As Marina approached the fence, Jennie dropped the small plastic rake she'd been carrying. She clutched the vinyl-covered wire with small fingers and tried to climb the fence. "Whatcha doin'? Me come."

"I'm planting bulbs. Do you know what bulbs are?" Marina opened the gate and came around to Jennie's side, gently disengaging the child from the fence before she fell.

Jennie shook her head in response to the question as she allowed Marina to take her hand. "I see? I p'ant bulbs?"

"Let's go ask Daddy if you can come over and help me plant some," Marina suggested. The feel of Jennie's trusting little hand in hers was a wonder that almost burst her hungry heart. To cover her emotion, she turned to practical matters. "Always ask Daddy first if you want to leave your yard. He might worry if he looked around and couldn't find you." As she started across the lawn toward Ben's house with Jennie, Major came to greet her, barking enthusiastically.

"Major, heel," Marina said sharply. When the dog obeyed immediately, her voice warmed with approval. "Good boy!"

"Amazing," said a masculine voice. "How do you do that?"

Marina smiled uncomfortably, regretting her lack of caution. Ben stood on his terrace with a leaf rake in his hand. His short-sleeved shirt revealed taut biceps and muscled forearms liberally covered with dark hair. How could forearms be so sexy? He must have come around from the far side of the yard in time to hear her. "Just luck, I guess," she hedged as she halted a short distance from him.

"Luck." Ben snorted, pointing with the end of the rake. "Look at him now. He never does that for me."

Marina glanced down. When she'd stopped, Major had obligingly settled his hindquarters to the ground in an automatic sit that any well-trained animal would know. Anxious to change the focus of the conversation, she chucked the dog under the chin and told him, "Go play, Major."

With a happy bark, the dog raced off.

She looked back at Ben with a smile, intending to ask about Jennie, who was still clinging to her right hand, but Ben was frowning at her.

"How did you know to do that?" His tone was almost bewildered.

She widened her eyes. "What? You mean release him? It's one of the first things they teach in canine obedience."

"I know that." Ben gestured after the animal distractedly. "But different owners vary the wording they use to release the dog. Most people release their dogs by saying 'Okay.' 'Go play' is a unique phrase my wife chose—I've never heard anyone else say it."

"Really?" She made her voice sound as casual as she could. "What a coincidence. I say 'Okay' in conversation too much. My dog was always getting up when he wasn't supposed to." Deliberately she looked down at Jennie. "I came over to ask if Jennie could help me for a little while. I'm planting bulbs in the backyard."

Ben nodded, but she could see that he was still puzzling over the incident with the dog. *Sugar!* She was as careful as she could be, but she seemed to arouse some concern in him with everything she did.

It was impossible for her to watch every phrase that came out of her mouth or every gesture that she made.

Ben knelt before Jennie. "I only have a few more leaves to rake and then it will be lunchtime. You can help Marina until I come to get you, okay?"

"'Tay." Jennie nodded solemnly. Then she tugged on Marina's hand with all her might. "Let's go!"

"Thanks. See you in a while." Marina forced herself to turn away casually from Ben and walk back to her yard with Jennie. Although her maternal nature gloried in this chance to spend time with her daughter, she also longed to stay with Ben.

But she couldn't. And she was darned lucky to have these few moments with Jennie, she reminded herself. Better quit moping and make the most of them.

Jennie was a delight in the time they spent digging holes and placing the daffodil bulbs in them. Marina marveled constantly at the things she'd learned in less than half a year. They were finishing the daffodils and starting on the last row of tulips when heels tapping on the flagstone path that led from the front of the house drew Marina's attention.

She looked up to see Jillian settling herself on a patio chair that Marina hadn't put away yet. Jillian was dressed as if she, too, had been to church.

"Hey, Earth Mother!" Jillian surveyed her sister with a smile that took any sting from the teasing name. "Dare I ask what you're doing?"

"Planting bulbs so I'll have some flowers to brighten the soggy spring days," Marina answered.

She gestured to Jennie, who had stopped digging and crept close to her side. "Do you remember my friend Jennie?"

"I certainly do." Jillian smiled at the little girl. "I saw you when you and your daddy came to visit our store. I'm Jillian. Do you remember me?"

Jennie nodded. One small thumb slipped into her mouth.

Marina rubbed the child's back encouragingly and ignored the fact that the thumb was covered with dirt. "Jennie saw lots of things in the store that she'd like Santa Claus to bring." To Jennie, she said, "Which one was your favorite?"

One little arm curled around Marina's left leg as Jennie lisped, "B'oo baby." Then she hid her face against Marina's black jeans.

Marina hesitated, then reached down and held out her arms. Jennie scooted forward and clung to her neck, apparently choosing her as a reliable source of security. Marina squeezed her eyes shut for a second as she lifted the little girl, absorbing the feel of the small arms winding around her neck. Tears threatened. How she'd missed this!

Jillian smiled and nodded at Jennie, oblivious to Marina's internal turmoil. "I like that one, too."

Marina forced herself to smile. It was obvious her sister hadn't a clue as to what Jennie had said. "The blue baby doll with the pacifier? That's a beautiful doll, Jennie. Maybe Santa will put that baby under your tree this year."

A bark from the direction of Ben's house stopped

her. Major bounded through the gate Ben had just
opened and came barreling toward her. Ben had his
back to her, closing the gate, so she made a hasty
hand signal and accompanied it with a quiet, "Down,
Major."

The dog dropped to the ground three paces from
her, tongue lolling and ears perked forward as he gave
her his complete attention.

Ben turned and walked across the lawn. "Have you
bewitched my dog again, Marina?" Then he spotted
Jill. "Hello, Jillian. Nice to see you. Did you come
to help with the planting?"

"It's nice to see you, too, Ben." Jillian batted her
eyes at Ben as she imbued the words with seductive
meaning. Then she broke the pose and laughed at herself. "And the answer's no. I wouldn't be caught dead
digging in the ground with these pampered digits."
She held up ten perfectly manicured nails.

Ben grinned and nodded. "I know what you mean.
People either love gardening or they hate it. I mow
the grass only because I don't want the neighbors to
complain. But my wife had the greenest thumb
you've ever seen. All Carrie had to do was look at a
seed and it sprouted. She loved this kind of thing."
He swept his arm out to encompass Marina's efforts.

Marina assessed him as he spoke to Jill. Did he
realize he'd mentioned Carrie's name without flinch-
ing? Marina had come to understand that the hesita-
tion that usually preceded Carrie's name was Ben's
way of steeling himself to deal with his feelings. Perhaps the first wave of raw grief was lessening a bit.

Then a thought struck her as she watched Ben laugh and joke with her sister. Could Ben be attracted to Jill, just as he'd been to her? Almost instantly she rejected the idea, but her mind kept creating imaginary scenarios in which Ben fell for her bubbly, bouncy, beautiful little sister...only because he was lonely, of course. He still loved Carrie. Didn't he?

It was frightening to realize how important the answer to that question was.

Ben could never be hers again.

She came back to reality with a start when she heard Jillian utter her name.

"...and at one time, I'd have said you were crazy if you'd told me Marina loved to garden. But here she is, living proof that a person can change." Jillian gestured to Marina, and Ben swung his gaze her way. "Of course, I realize her situation is rather unusual. Not too many people get a knock in the head that permanently alters their behavior."

"Not too many...." Ben murmured encouragingly, grinning unrepentantly at Marina when she frowned.

It was all Jill needed. "I mean, the doctors warned me that even a minor head injury can cause personality changes, but Marina has been a totally different person since the accident. She loves animals, she loves fooling with plants, she doesn't mind getting messy...even her food tastes have changed." She shook her head and turned to smile at Marina. "Not that I'm complaining, mind you. I feel so glad you survived that I'll take you with any quirks you can name!"

Marina forced herself to laugh lightly. "Careful—you could be eating those words."

"Actually, I had some lunch in mind." Jill grinned. "Can I bum a meal?"

"I suppose so. Let me clean up my things here." She shifted Jennie on her hip and, unable to resist, brushed a kiss over the silky dark hair. "Thanks for helping me plant my bulbs, Jennie. We'll have some beautiful flowers to look at in the springtime."

Ben held out his hand to his daughter. "It's time for lunch, Jennie. Tell Marina, 'Thank you.'"

Jennie turned her face away and tightened her arms in a stranglehold on Marina's neck. "I have lunch wif M'rina." The words were muffled in Marina's neck, but the belligerence in the tone came through clearly.

Jillian covered her mouth with a hand to hide her smile.

Marina looked helplessly over Jennie's head at Ben, who stepped forward and patted his daughter's back. Bending his head down to where Jennie's face was buried against Marina, he said, "Some other day, maybe. Today Marina and her sister have lots of grown-up things to talk about and she can't play with you."

Jennie's grip didn't loosen even a fraction. "I no' go! 'Tay wif M'rina."

"Not now, Peanut. But I'll make you a deal. If you come eat lunch with me now, you can ask Marina to play at our house after your nap and eat supper with us tonight."

Jennie lifted her head and eyed her father. "After nap?"

"Uh-huh." Ben nodded affirmatively.

The little girl's palms lifted to Marina's cheeks and she looked straight into her face as she asked, "You come play wif me after nap?"

Marina managed a nod. Her voice was tight as she rested her forehead against Jennie's for an instant. "I'd love to, Jen. I'll see you later, okay?"

"Otay." Satisfied now, Jennie wriggled down and ran off across the yard.

"Thanks," Ben said. "About four would be fine."

"Four it is. What can I bring?" She didn't really want to be alone with Ben—she'd bet he wanted to question her about the accident and her memory loss. But she wouldn't disappoint Jennie for the world.

Ben shrugged. "Whatever. A salad?"

When she nodded, he waved. "See you later, then." Then he turned to Jillian. "I'll be in to the store for some help with my Christmas shopping."

Jillian smiled. "We have some wonderful toys this year. Don't wait too late."

Ben followed Jennie back to the gate, but halfway there, he turned and called, "May I have my dog back now?"

Marina gave a startled groan. Major lay in the same spot she'd put him, still watching her. With a chagrined smile for Ben, she released the animal from his down-stay. "Good boy, Major. Go to Ben."

Jillian was shaking her head in bemusement when Marina turned to pick up her gardening tools.

"Where did you learn to do that?"

Marina shrugged as she opened the back door and placed her things on a table in the screened porch before entering the house. "It's easy, really," she said. "Major's a well-trained animal who just happens to respond to me exceptionally well. I'm training Lucky, too." The dog in question leapt around their feet as they went into the kitchen. Jillian set her purse on the table while Marina washed her hands.

"Your handsome neighbor seems quite taken with you," Jill commented, idly tracing the leaf of a trailing ivy vine that spilled from a shelf near the window.

"He's just being friendly." Did she sound too defensive?

"More than 'friendly,' sister dear. The man is definitely interested in you." Jillian raised her gaze, and her teasing expression turned remorseful when she saw the anxiety that Marina couldn't hide. "I'm sorry. I didn't mean to upset you. I know it's too soon to be thinking of new relationships." She came around the table and massaged Marina's shoulders lightly.

What should she say to that? Afraid to even attempt to discuss Ben, she finally settled on the one thing she did want Jillian to understand. Walking away from her sister's hands, she crossed to the opposite counter and turned, clasping her arms across her chest defensively. "Jill, I'd appreciate it if you didn't discuss my accident—or anything about my life—with people who didn't know me then." She knew it wasn't fair to blame Jillian for the earlier conversation, but she wanted to be sure her sister understood. Ben had been deliberately prying. He'd practically laughed in her face about it, too.

Jillian's eyes rounded. "You mean you haven't told Ben about the accident...or your memory?"

"No."

Slowly Jillian slumped into a chair, her long, elegant legs folded beneath her. "Wow." She turned stricken blue eyes to Marina. "I'm sorry. I had no idea. I assumed he knew, or I never would have said a word."

She mimed sealing her lips, then immediately began to talk again. Marina smiled ruefully as Jill launched into the next thing that occurred to her. "So why are you keeping him in the dark? You've obviously gotten to be friends."

Marina shrugged. "I just don't think that everyone I meet needs to know about my past. It's irrelevant now."

Jillian studied her for a moment. "Marina...how do I say this? You were a great person before. Don't get me wrong. But you were very different. Is that what's bugging you? You think Ben's not going to be attracted if he finds out you weren't a happy homemaker before the accident?"

Marina was astounded. "Oh, Jill—" She stopped short as laughter choked her. "With an imagination like that, you're missing your calling."

Now Jillian was on the defensive. "I thought it was a plausible explanation," she said in a huffy tone.

"After all, devoted to Ron though you were, you've never been the hearth-and-home type."

"Is that what I am now?"

Jillian gestured around at the plants, the cheerful red and yellow accents in the kitchen, the white cat that occupied the chair next to hers; finally she pointed at the dog who had settled himself on the red rug near the back door. "Now you're a person I can imagine as a mother."

"What's that supposed to mean?"

"I could never envision you with children of your own. You always seemed too...too perfect to get dirty or something. Now..." Jill shrugged and spread her hands "...you're more approachable, more human."

Marina's mouth quirked. "Are you trying to tell me I'm messy?" Then she sobered. "Is that why Ron and I never had any children? Didn't I want kids?"

"Oh, that wasn't it." Jill searched Marina's face. "You really don't remember anything, do you?" It was a rhetorical question and she went on as if it required no answer. "You both wanted children in the worst way, and after a few years of trying with no luck, you two consulted a specialist. Ron was tested first and the reason showed up right away. The doctor couldn't say why, but Ron was sterile."

"Sterile?"

"Right. As far as I know, you're fine, but Ron could never father children."

"How sad. Were we very disappointed?" Marina could imagine how she'd feel if she were given such news.

"You hid it well." Jillian pursed her lips and blew back a strand of silky blond hair. "Ron was very depressed initially, but I think it was partly because he was afraid you'd take it badly."

"And did I?"

Jill snorted. "Are you kidding? You were wonderful—built up his ego, discussed adoption—you never mentioned biological children again. You were on the verge of applying to a private adoption agency when the accident happened."

Marina stared off into space for a moment. Finally she shook herself and looked across the table at her sister. "I can't imagine how I must have felt. I can't imagine never having the chance to bear a child."

Ben braced himself when he heard the doorbell ring later that afternoon. Although he'd shamelessly used Jennie as a pretext for seeing Marina again, he still felt guilty for craving her company.

And crave it he did. He'd missed her in the past couple of weeks. They'd only spent a handful of minutes together in the time he'd known her, and yet he found himself wanting to share things with her, to tell her amusing anecdotes about Jennie, to ask her opinion on the Christmas ideas he was beginning to consider. Even though part of him wanted to crawl in a hole and hibernate at the thought of spending the holidays without Carrie, he was determined to make them happy for Jennie's sake.

He pulled open the door, and as always, Marina's sheer beauty struck him like a punch in the gut, making his breath come fast and shallow. Her wide blue eyes were deep, mysterious pools of color. Combined with the pink of her cheeks and lips, the combination gave her the look of an angel.

When she took off her black coat, he was stunned even more. The jeans she'd worn today had fit like a second skin. Tonight she wore an oversize sweater in navy and gold with navy stretch pants that hugged her long slender legs. The sweater caught her at mid-thigh, offering tempting glances of her shapely bottom as she turned to pick up the bowl she had placed on a side table.

"Hi." Was that his voice? He sounded like he'd just awakened from a three-day binge.

"Hi. Here's a gelatin salad." She handed him the bowl. "It should be refrigerated unless we're eating right away."

Ben stepped aside and motioned for her to precede him into the family room. "I thought we'd eat around five, if that's not too early for you. Jennie took a nap earlier than usual today and she'll probably be ready for bed by seven."

"That's fine." She immediately headed for the couch where Jennie was sitting holding her shoes in her lap.

"Watch it," Ben cautioned softly as he turned to take the salad to the kitchen. "She woke up in the mother-and-father of a bad mood."

As he placed the salad in the refrigerator, he took one quick peek. Strawberry salad! Now how had she known that was one of his favorites? It looked exactly like the kind Carrie used to make and his mouth watered just looking at it. He preset the oven so he could begin to bake the chicken he'd prepared earlier, then strode back into the family room to rescue Marina from Jennie the Grump.

Jennie was sitting on Marina's lap. Her shoes—the ones she'd refused to let him help her put on—were on her feet and Marina was halfway through Jennie's favorite story.

Quietly he sank into a chair, enjoying the few minutes of peace. Being a single parent was hell. When he and Jennie clashed, as was inevitable even on the best of days, there was no one else to act as a buffer, no one who wasn't exhausted from dealing with a two-year-old all day to step in and smooth out the wrinkles in their relationship or simply to distract and redirect her. He loved Jennie more than anything in the world, but interaction with someone else was good for them both.

Marina gave Jennie her sole attention until dinnertime, reading stories and getting down on the floor to build houses with interlocking blocks, rocking Jennie's babies and playing doctor at the child's request. She'd obviously taken him at his word when he'd invited her over to play with Jennie.

They had a family-style meal in the kitchen because Marina insisted that he go to no extra work. Afterward she offered to bathe Jennie while he cleaned up the kitchen. He showed her where the towels, tub toys and clean pajamas were kept and left her to it, marveling at how capable she was for someone who'd never been around small children much.

By the time he'd finished with the dishes, Jennie came padding out in her footed pajamas for a good-night kiss. When he offered to read her a story, she told him, "M'rina read." Smiling quizzically, he shook his head in denial when Marina asked him if he'd like to read. They sat in the family room for the story, then Jennie demanded that Marina put her to bed.

Fifteen minutes later, Marina sank down onto the sofa in the family room. "Whew! I forgot how hard children play. That was work."

Ben grinned as he crossed the room to turn on the monitor that would allow him to hear Jennie if she cried out. "I guess you don't usually interact with them to this extent at the store."

"No. I rarely spend more than a few minutes with a child." Regret clearly laced her voice.

"You were a godsend to me tonight. It's tough to try to be all things to a child, especially one as young as Jennie." He lifted his arms above his head in a mighty stretch. "How about a glass of wine? It'll take the kinks out."

When Marina hesitated, he added, "I'm going to have one."

"All right. Thank you."

He hurried into the kitchen before she could change her mind and returned a moment later with two fluted goblets filled with white wine. Sinking down onto the couch a safe distance from her, he handed her one, holding his own in the traditional toast gesture.

Marina leaned forward, holding hers in a similar manner.

Ben hesitated, searching for the right words. "To surviving what life throws at us, and to friendship."

"To friendship," Marina echoed in a husky tone as the clear chime of crystal rang out. She settled back against the corner of the couch, kicking off her shoes and propping her feet on his battered coffee table. "Do you mind?" she asked.

"Not at all," Ben said with a wave of his hand. "That table has taken a lot worse treatment than your feet can dish out."

Marina smiled. "I can't believe that sweet little girl sleeping in there would destroy your furniture."

"Not on purpose." Ben laughed. "But you'd be amazed at the thumps and bumps that go on in here when Jennie's dragging her babies around in a carriage. And she doesn't take it well when I ask her to stop."

"Is it difficult?" Marina's voice was sympathetic. "Being an only parent, I mean."

Ben exhaled on a deep sigh. "I was thinking about that earlier when you were reading to Jen. I love her, but yeah, it's a real drain being the only person on call all day. There are actually days when I'm thankful that I have to work because I know I'm going to get a break!"

Marina chuckled. "I can't imagine that. She's so precious. Just send her over anytime you need a break.'' She slouched lower against the back of the couch and crossed her legs at the ankle where they rested atop the low table. ''I never get tired of the children that come into the store.''

''How about your sister? Does she like children?''

''Loves 'em. But she's dedicated herself to finding the perfect man before she starts procreating.''

''Wise woman.'' Ben swirled his wine idly. ''So Kerr was your maiden name?'' Was it his imagination, or did Marina tense a little at the question?

''Uh-huh.''

''Were your parents from around here?''

''My dad was. He grew up in St. Mary's. But he met my mom at college. She was from North Carolina.''

''Do you have any other family besides your sister?''

''Uh, no. No cousins or anything. Just Jillian.''

''Just Jillian,'' he repeated. He remembered what Jillian had said about Marina's accident earlier, and he could restrain his curiosity no longer as he thought of the man named Jerry and his comment in the shop last weekend. ''I didn't realize you were involved in, uh, the accident. Jillian spoke as if you were injured when she talked about it today.''

''I wasn't hurt badly. Just a bump on the head.''

''She claims it altered your behavior.'' No question about it, Marina was definitely uptight about this topic. He wondered if it was grief or something else that was upsetting her. To distract her, he picked up a flat pillow and tossed it at her. "Mind if I stretch out?"

"N-no." As the pillow landed in her lap, she slid over another inch or two toward the end of the couch.

"Stay still." Leaning toward her, he shifted so that he could lay his feet on the pillow in her lap with his body reclining. His head was propped on the far arm of the long sofa. "So tell me about your memory loss."

Marina's eyes opened very wide. "My...memory loss?"

"If you really don't want to talk about it, we won't," he said gently. "But I heard what that guy said in the store and I'd like to know what happened. I'm your friend, remember?"

"My friend," she echoed. The room was silent and he could sense the struggle going on inside her. He wished he could read her mind. He badly wanted to know more about her and his words had been a deliberate gamble. If she rebuffed him, he'd have to back off. And he found he wasn't ready to do that. He needed a friend as badly as he believed she did.

"According to Jillian, my husband Ron and I were boating on the Chesapeake," she began. Her words riveted his attention. *According to Jillian...?* He remained quiet as she went on, describing what Jillian had told her about the accident and the ensuing events.

"...and the doctors say I'll probably never regain my memory," she finished.

Ben was incredulous. How could thirty-odd years

of someone's life be wiped out like that? "Are you sure? Have you had a second opinion?"

"And a third and a fourth," Marina said tiredly. "I don't want to be a medical freak. I just want to get on with my life. I'm in perfect health."

The concept of her amnesia was intriguing. "But Jillian says you've changed radically, to her mind."

"I know. The doctors say that persons who have suffered head injuries sometimes find even their basic personality traits altered. I have no way of knowing exactly how much I've changed, but it appears to be very...disturbing...for her."

Ben fell silent, not knowing what to say to that. Marina had been holding her wineglass in her right hand; now she rested it on the wide, flat expanse of the pillow.

At the feel of the cold side of the goblet on his stockinged foot, Ben was abruptly jolted out of his languor and catapulted into the past. He'd lain on this sofa many nights in the past, only Carrie's lap had been the place his head rested then, and her fingers had played in his hair.

It was the damnedest thing, he mused, how a woman who looked like such a femme fatale could project a homey, comforting presence so much like his wife had. He'd often teased Carrie about her nesting instinct, her knack for taking any surroundings and turning them into an intimate setting. In some indefinable manner, Marina was able to do the same thing.

Or perhaps it wasn't so indefinable. When Jennie

had been fussing about eating lunch with her, Marina had looked over her head at him much as Carrie had used to, plainly saying, "This issue needs to be addressed by Daddy." It was almost as if he was with Carrie when Marina was near. He had to bite down hard on the impulse to blurt out an invitation to dinner—without Jennie along.

If anyone had told him a year ago that Carrie would be dead and buried and he'd be contemplating asking out another woman less than six months later, he'd have said they needed a shrink. He could hardly believe it himself. But he desperately wanted to ask Marina for a date.

No way. Back off, Bradford. He couldn't think of a less-flattering reason to ask a woman out. If Marina found out that he wanted to date her because she reminded him of his wife, she'd be less than thrilled. She'd probably be furious. And hurt.

She was so soft, so gentle. He couldn't bear the thought of hurting her when she'd been so good to him, so good *for* him. Grimly he shoved aside the sexual interest that his thoughts were fueling. She was a friend, nothing more, and he wanted to keep it that way. Dating was a lousy idea. Neither of them could be ready for another relationship.

Could they?

He needed her, but only as a friend. He could control his urges.

Couldn't he?

Five

Marina watched Ben as he gazed into space, her mind still engrossed in how she could allay his interest in her amnesia. Had he sensed evasion in her carefully worded answers to his queries?

Even though she hadn't outright lied to him, she was immensely uncomfortable with any form of dissembling. Her beyond-death experience, which was how she'd come to define it, had altered her life in many ways, but one point was clear. Every moment of every day of the rest of the life she now lived as Marina Devereaux had to be the very best she could make it.

As Carrie Bradford, she thought she'd been a pretty decent person. But she'd been guilty of many petty little emotions—envy, jealousy, superiority—emotions that she now recognized there was no room for in her life.

That thought made her lips curve up in a slight smile. It was almost amusing to think that there was something she had no time for in her life. The days were a quiet blend of satisfying work at the store and long, lonely moments puttering around her home. She had no real purpose except a faint hope of seeing Ben and Jennie from day to day.

He was so quiet now. She wondered what was going on in that lightning-quick brain of his. Absently she lifted her wineglass to her lips and sipped.

"Have I told you how much I'm coming to value our friendship?"

She jumped slightly as Ben's voice broke the silence. "Umm, no," she replied.

"Well, I am. I feel as if we've known each other much longer than a few weeks."

Oh, Ben, if only you knew. "I feel the same way."

"We're good for each other. It's been comforting to me to be able to share my feelings with someone who's going through the same thing."

"Yes. It's made my life bearable." *But not for the reasons you imagine.* Then Marina forced herself to laugh a little. "Sort of like our own exclusive therapy group."

"Yeah." Ben laughed, too, and his wine sloshed dangerously. "Whoa. Carrie used to use me for a table when we sat and talked after dinner. Once I sneezed and we both got soaked in Chablis."

She remembered that spill. And even worse, she

remembered them helping each other to discard their wine-soiled clothing, Ben tasting the wine on her skin, the slick, soapy shower they'd taken together to clean up. The images it brought to mind fired her body with a futile longing so strong she was afraid he would sense the need boiling within her if she didn't get out of his presence.

Abruptly she lifted the glass and drained it, then pushed his feet off her lap so fast he almost fell off the couch. "I'd better get going. We're preparing for Christmas at the shop and it'll be a long day tomorrow."

Ben frowned as he recovered his balance. "Do you always work so hard?"

"I don't know." The bald answer sounded slightly wistful, even to her.

To her relief, he didn't comment, but reached over and gripped her hand in a clasp that spoke of comfort and caring.

Then, in a lithe move that reminded her of how fast he could move when it suited him, he rolled to his feet and held out his hands to pull her up. When she would have drawn her hands away, he tucked one into the crook of his elbow and strolled with her toward the door. He was big and warm beside her, a tantalizing torment. She wanted him so...she was almost frantic to get away before she spoiled everything by kissing him with all the pent-up need she'd harbored since July.

At the door, he retrieved her coat and held it while she put her arms into the sleeves. Then he handed her the salad bowl he'd washed and set on the table in the foyer. When he opened the door, crisp November wind swirled in as a cold front chased the warm weather away. Marina shivered.

Ben smiled and the warmth in his eyes reached deep into her heart. "Thanks for coming tonight."

Marina nodded. "Thanks for inviting me." She wanted to move, meant to move. But Ben's gaze was searching hers—looking for what? As his face drew closer, she closed her eyes, helplessly clutching the salad bowl, waiting...waiting...waiting for the touch of his lips on hers.

His big hands settled on her shoulders, drawing her close until her knuckles, curved around the bowl, were pressed into his hard chest. She felt the warmth of his wine-scented breath on her face. Then, gently, he rubbed his nose back and forth, back and forth, against the tip of hers. Her lips ached for contact, but she was too mesmerized to tilt her face up. Despite her disappointment, it was an outrageously intimate act that shot quivers of liquid heat through her. In some odd way, the tender touching was as erotic as if he'd kissed her with all the graphic sensuality of which she knew he was capable.

"Good night." His voice was a husky whisper as he drew back a scant distance.

"Good night." She turned and fled.

The week was a busy one for Marina. Thanksgiving was only seven days away and after that, Kids' Place would be in the swing of Christmas. Already they were getting orders and requests for special items.

On Thursday, Marina was pulling her car out of the driveway when she noticed Ben doing the same thing. He waved at her. Then, stopping before he pulled out of his driveway, he got out and came toward her.

"Hi." She rolled her window down and absorbed the power of his long strides as he crossed the lawn between them. Every time she was near him, she was conscious of deliberately making memories, storing away images of everything he did and said in case the day came that she could no longer see him.

"Hi. How're you feeling?" He grasped the sill of her car window and leaned down to her height.

Marina thought it an odd greeting. "Fine. Any reason?"

Ben grinned ruefully. "Jennie came down with some sort of flu bug on Tuesday. I thought I'd better warn you since you were exposed to her on Sunday. I'm hoping that if we haven't gotten it by now, we won't."

"Amen." Marina returned the smile. Then she looked toward his house. "Are you taking time off work?"

Ben shook his head. "No. Mom came over here so I wouldn't have to take Jen out of the house. It's just a minor rearrangement of our schedule." He hesitated. "Do you have plans for Saturday evening?"

Marina shook her head, her pulse jumping at the possibility of spending more time with him. "No. I'd planned on working most of the day, but it's not definite yet. We give our part-time help more hours at Christmas, so I can go in whenever I want.''

"Good. I thought maybe we could do dinner again if Jennie's better. She really enjoyed playing with you the other night.''

"And I enjoyed her every bit as much.'' Marina was thrilled by the invitation, even if it had been issued for Jennie's sake. "I'd love to have dinner with the Bradfords again.''

"Okay. It's a date.'' Ben lightly slapped the edge of her window. "See you Saturday.''

"See you Saturday.'' She should have said no, pleaded another engagement, anything to avoid spending another evening in his company. But she hadn't.

And she wouldn't. Marina knew exactly how much willpower she had. Resisting Ben's charm wasn't something she was equipped to do.

On Saturday morning, the telephone awakened her from a sound sleep. Reaching for the cordless receiver, she noted that it wasn't quite seven yet, and her heart began to pound. Jillian was the only person she could think of who'd call her this early. What could be the matter?

She sat up and pushed her hair out of her eyes. "Hello?''

"Marina. It's Ben. Sorry to bother you so early.''

Ben! Although her heart skipped a beat, she was alarmed by the slurred quality of his voice. "Is something wrong?''

"Yeah.'' He groaned and she shot out of bed, already reaching for a pair of jeans. "I've got the flu. Mom's sick, too, and I don't have anyone to watch Jennie. Could I impose on you today?"

"Of course." She hopped around, trying to stuff her legs into her pants. "Just let me throw on some clothes and I'll be over."

"Okay." There was a ragged sigh from the other end of the line. "Thanks."

"Sure. See you in a few minutes."

Hanging up the phone, she flew into a turquoise sweatshirt, socks and sneakers, then gave herself a hasty once-over in the bathroom before grabbing her coat and racing out the door.

When she got to Ben's house, the front door wasn't locked. As she stepped inside, Jennie came bouncing down the hallway from the family room. "Daddy sick! Daddy sick!"

Ben was behind her, wearing a pair of worn navy sweatpants and a T-shirt. She knew he didn't own a pair of pajamas. His face was as white as the socks she'd just donned, his hair a spiked sensation. He was positively weaving on his feet.

Marina rushed toward him. "What are you doing out of bed?"

"Thought I could manage. Jennie's breakfast...."

"I'll do that." She slipped an arm around him and steered him in the direction of the bedroom, alarmed at the heat radiating from him. "You're burning up. Have you taken anything?"

"Haven't tried since last night. I couldn't keep anything down for a while."

They had reached the bedroom doorway and she glanced at the bed, hoping the covers were already drawn back. The bed—her bed—was gone! She stopped dead. Beside her, Ben stopped, too, clutching at the doorframe for additional support. He didn't comment and it flashed through her mind that he probably thought she was giving him a rest.

Where had her bed gone? Stifling the question was nearly more than she could manage. She bit down on her bottom lip so hard she tasted blood. She'd loved the gleaming brass bed that she and Ben had purchased right before their marriage. Her wedding night had been spent in that bed. Jennie had been conceived there.

Now a wooden bed of light oak occupied the place of her beloved bed. It was a handsome piece of furniture, she supposed, but it wasn't her bed. The discovery had thrown her completely off balance. She started in surprise when Ben said, "Okay, I can make it now."

Gathering her scattered emotions, she helped him across the room. *Don't think about the bed. Just think about why you're here—a neighbor lending a helping hand.*

"Do you feel nauseous now?" Despite her preoccupation, she was relieved when he sank onto the bed. If he'd passed out, she'd have had a hard time moving him. She might have gained a few inches, but Ben still outweighed her by nearly a hundred pounds.

"No. I think it may have passed."

Pulling the covers all the way back, she lifted his

feet onto the bed, then covered him. "I know you feel warm, but try to keep covered. I'll be back in a minute with some medicine."

Unhesitating, she turned and headed for the cabinet in the kitchen where she kept all the medications—where she knew Ben kept all the medications, she corrected herself. It was lucky that he was too sick to wonder at how she knew where to find the stuff she needed.

Jennie was following her from place to place and she took time to scoop up the child and carry her along. "So you gave Daddy and Gramma the flu, did you?" she asked. "You'll have to help me take good care of Daddy until he's all better."

There was a bowl on the counter, but Ben hadn't managed to get any cereal into it. Quickly Marina got Jennie some breakfast and installed her at the kitchen table. "I'll be back after I give Daddy some medicine," she told the tot. "You eat your cereal and then maybe you and I will go down to my store. Would you like that, dollbaby?"

"Uh-huh!" Jennie waved her spoon enthusiastically.

Carrying a bucket, a large glass of ice water and a bottle of medicine that she hoped would reduce Ben's fever, she returned to the bedroom. "Here," she said as she approached the bed—and repressed the urge to question him about it. "Let's see if a little of this will stay in your stomach. It should help bring down that fever."

Ben's eyes were glassy and he made feeble shooing motions. "Get out of here before you catch this."

"I never get sick," she said smugly.

"There's a first time for everything," he croaked as he sat up and drained the medicine spoon, then took a sip of the water.

"That's not a nice thing to say to your angel of mercy," she reproved as she fluffed the pillow, then repositioned it behind him.

"You're right." He flopped back down. "Thanks. I really appreciate this, Marina."

She closed the drapes when she noticed he was wincing at the light, then pulled up the covers to his chest and sat on the side of his bed. "I know. You can return the favor sometime." She indicated the bucket. "I brought this along, just in case."

Ben shuddered. "I don't think I'll need it again. Guess time will tell."

Remembering what he'd said about his mother, she wondered if she should stop by and check on her, as well. "Is Helen as sick as you are?"

Ben nodded, his eyelids sinking down. "She was yesterday. That was when she called and told me she'd caught the flu."

"Would you like me to see how she's doing?"

His eyes opened a crack. "That's awfully nice of you, but I think she'll be all right. One of her friends was going to stay with her. I'll call her later when I'm feeling a little better."

"Or I'll do it if you're still down for the count." She prepared to rise, but he caught her hand.

"Marina, sorry about dinner. We'll have to post-pone it."

"Another time will be fine." She was acutely conscious of the intimacy of their position, her hip pressed into the curve of his body. Even if the man was sicker than a dog, his face devoid of color and shadowed by beard stubble, he still raised her blood pressure. "Will it be okay if I take Jennie down to the store for a little while? We won't be long."

"S'okay by me." He raised her hand to his cheek. "Will you check in on me when you get back?" He sounded lonely and pathetic, and she had to smile. Ben had never handled illness well.

"Of course." She couldn't resist turning her palm over and caressing his cheek for an instant. "Rest now."

He nodded, his intense dark gaze clinging to hers, though his eyelids were drooping. "You're one special lady. I'm glad you came into my life."

Ben awoke slowly, as groggy as if he'd slept for weeks. He turned his head cautiously to look at the digital clock on the nightstand, expecting a return of the stabbing pain he'd endured throughout the night...and was pleasantly surprised when no sharp-toothed monster leapt at his nerve endings.

His eyes focused on the clock face. Two o'clock. Afternoon. He wondered where Jennie and Marina were. He had a vague memory of Marina promising to look in on him, and mild irritation rose. She obviously hadn't bothered.

Almost as fast as the thought formed, he was ashamed. His neighbor was a busy professional with her own business to run, and he'd imposed on her to baby-sit as if she had nothing better to do. She'd been more than gracious about it, but he couldn't take advantage of that longer than was absolutely necessary.

Well, he'd get on his feet, let her see that he could cope, and thank her on her way out the door. Game plan established, he rolled to a standing position beside the bed—

—and crumpled abruptly when his knees turned to jelly and the room swam around him. "Damn*nation*." He put his hands to his head, hoping to keep the calliope inside from spinning so vigorously.

When the room finally stilled around him, he cautiously dropped his hands. Inching to the foot of the bed, he grabbed hold of the beveled post at the corner of the footboard. So far, so good. Now, if he could stay on his feet until the dizziness passed, he'd be just fine.

"Ben Bradford, what do you think you're doing?" Marina advanced into the room, her tone clearly less than pleased.

Hoping she didn't realize what an effort his actions required, he hauled himself to his feet again and stood facing her, clinging to the bedpost. "I know you have things you need to do," he began. "And I'm feeling much better, so you can leave anytime you like."

"Are you trying to tell me to scram?" she asked softly, and he saw hurt in her steady gaze. "If you really want me to leave, I will, but I don't think you're ready to be Daddy-in-Charge yet. You look as if you're about to drop. Besides, I enjoy Jennie. This is probably the closest I'll ever get to motherhood." She looked away then, but before she did, he saw something raw, something so painful in the depths of her eyes he could hardly bear to be a witness to it.

His legs were quivering and he sat near the corner of the bed. "You said you'd check in on me." As soon as the words popped out, he felt ridiculous.

"And I did, as soon as Jennie and I came back from the shop." Urging him to turn slightly away from her, she put her hands on his shoulders and began to massage. He grunted in approval. How had she known that he was one big ache? "You were sleeping, so Jennie and I had lunch and then I read to her and put her down for a nap. She's still sleeping."

At the word "Lunch," his stomach gave an embarrassing growl.

Marina laughed. "Do you think you could keep down some soup?"

"Yeah." Soup sounded great. "There's some canned soup in the pantry."

Her fingers tightened on and released his shoulders. "I made some chicken noodle soup this afternoon while Jennie was sleeping. I thought it might appeal to you."

He'd better keep his mouth shut or he'd drool. "Homemade chicken noodle soup?" He couldn't keep the note of hope from his voice.

"Homemade chicken noodle soup," she confirmed.

"I think I've died and gone to heaven."

She laughed, and there was genuine amusement in the sound. "I can guarantee you haven't."

She helped him into the bathroom and went off to dish up some of her soup. He brushed the fur off his teeth with real enthusiasm, then donned a sweatshirt for warmth before shuffling out to the kitchen.

Marina met him halfway. "I would have brought it for you," she said as she slipped an arm under his shoulder and around his back.

"No, it's good to be on my feet." Especially when she was so close, her breast pressing into his chest, her thighs cradling one of his as she helped him to a chair. God, he wished he felt better. She'd taste better than chicken noodle soup anyday.

The thought was mildly shocking. He'd been attracted to her since the day they'd met, but he hadn't intended to act on it. He'd felt too newly widowed for it not to be a sinful act.

Until now.

As he sipped at the hot soup she'd made, he thought about her. Admitting that he wanted Marina, that he'd like to make love to her, was easy. But thinking about the implications of what that meant was much more involved. Did he want to ask her out? He felt uneasy with the thought. But was it because he was genuinely not ready to be with her, or because he was worried about what the rest of the world might think?

It probably wasn't wise to get involved with anyone so soon after Carrie's death. Especially with the holidays coming up. This first Christmas without his wife was going to be hellish. It wouldn't be fair to use Marina to avoid facing the emptiness that the season was sure to create in him.

"Would you like to share Thanksgiving with Jennie, Helen and me?" Good God. He'd better not open his mouth again until he'd gained control over what came out of it. Hadn't he just decided not to ask her out?

Apparently there'd been a short circuit somewhere in his brain. Oh, well. Asking her to Thanksgiving dinner wasn't exactly a date.

When he dared to glance at her, she was looking thoughtful. "I'm not sure. I mean, thank you for the invitation. I'd like to come, but I'm not sure what happens at Thanksgiving. I'll have to check with Jillian and let you know."

He sobered as he remembered that she no memories of previous holidays. "You do know what Thanksgiving is?"

"Yes."

The monosyllable was subdued and he couldn't bring himself to question her further. It must be a terrible burden to reach into your memory and come away with—nothing.

"Thank you for joining us for Thanksgiving. Your presence made the day easier to get through." Helen Bradford extended her hand to Jillian after giving Marina a warm hug.

Ben watched with a smile, pleased that his mother

had been so gracious to his guests. It had been a surprisingly pleasant day. He'd dreaded the arrival of these holidays, had wished he could be an ostrich and bury his head in the sand until they'd passed.

But Marina and Jillian had kept the day light and relaxing, and Thanksgiving had passed without the haze of misery he'd expected to endure. As he walked across the grass to Marina's door with the sisters, he felt a pang of guilt that he hadn't grieved harder.

Jillian threw a friendly arm around his shoulders as they waited for Marina to dig out her house key. "Thanks for asking us to join you today. I haven't had such a good time at Thanksgiving in years." She gave him a droll wink. "Of course, I could have done without being bested at tiddledywinks by a two-year-old."

Ben laughed. "I forgot to warn you, the kid's a shark." He brushed a light kiss on Jill's cheek. "We were delighted that you came. It would have been a grim holiday without you two."

Marina flung open the door then, and they all trooped in, laden with the care packages of turkey and trimmings that Helen had insisted on sending home with Jillian and Marina. As Ben watched the two blondes pack up a basket for Jillian to carry home, he wondered idly why it was that attractive, vivacious Jillian didn't raise his blood pressure one iota, while her quieter sister could have his pulse pounding with a mere glance from the corner of her big blue eyes.

"Stop!" Jillian shook a finger at Marina. "You're

just sending all this pumpkin pie with me so I'm the one who'll have to diet after the holidays.''

Marina shrugged. ''I don't like pumpkin pie. Feed it to one of your many suitors.''

''But didn't you make this?'' Ben indicated the pie.

''Yeah, but I don't have to eat it.'' Marina wrinkled her nose.

''My wife was the same way,'' he said, struck once again by a sense of déjà vu. ''She made it for me every year, but she couldn't stand the thought of eating it.''

Jillian rolled her eyes in disbelief. ''This is one more way my sister has changed. She used to be the first one to sneak seconds on pumpkin pie when Mom wasn't looking. Now she doesn't even like it anymore.'' She shook her head in good-natured exasperation. ''It's a good thing I love you.''

Marina's eyes softened. ''I love you, too, Jill. Thanks for coming with me today.'' She embraced her sister, then drew away as Jillian turned to Ben.

''Thanks again for inviting us.'' Jill lifted the basket Marina handed her, pretending to stagger under its weight. ''Good night, all.''

Marina held open the door for her, then stood inside and watched until Jillian's car disappeared down the quiet street. Being alone with Ben was a bad idea. She was conscious of a trembling expectancy in the pit of her stomach, but she ignored it. Her hormones always stood at attention when Ben was near. That didn't mean he felt the same way. It *had* been a lovely day. She hated to see it end. Maybe it didn't have to, yet. "Would you like some coffee?" she asked Ben. "Or a drink?"

Ben shook his head. He'd been standing behind her, watching Jillian depart. "Not unless you're making something for yourself. Why don't we sit in the living room and talk? I love Jennie, but it's nice to hear nothing but an adult's soothing tones for once."

Marina laughed. "She does like the sound of her own voice, doesn't she?" She paused to let Lucky out into the backyard, then led the way into her living room, stopping in front of an elegant cream-and-gold flowered couch.

Ben whistled as he halted in the middle of the room and took in the gleaming glass-and-brass tables with their tasteful displays of silk flowers and fine-china accent pieces. "This is nice."

"And it would last about two minutes in your house." Marina shrugged her shoulders. "It was in the condo—from before the accident. I guess it's just one more way I've changed, because it's certainly not to my taste now." She moved again. "Would you like to see the rest of the place? I've put together a small den that I think you'll like better."

"It's not that I don't like it," Ben protested. "It's just that it's…"

"Fussy."

"Maybe a little."

"Let's see…" Marina ushered him across the front entryway. "You've seen the kitchen. Here's the dining room. More of the same, I'm afraid."

And it was. Ben had to agree with her. It was all

lovely but, except for the kitchen, it did seem fussy. Not at all what he'd expected from a warm, giving woman like Marina. Down a short hallway were three bedrooms. The first she skipped, saying that it was her office and that it was a disaster area.

A quick glance showed him that she was right.

The second was what she called her den. "I spend most of my time in here rather than in that living room," she told him as he surveyed it with approval. There was much more of her in here, he thought. Floor-to-ceiling shelving held a compact-disc player and tuner, a television and videocassette recorder, and books crammed into every available space. Pieces of comfortable furniture with blue fabric pillows were arranged around the edge of a rag rug. One basket held magazines and catalogs, another contained needlework, and the rug was scattered with several rubber toys he presumed were for her pets. On the walls were several large framed prints that he recognized as the cover illustrations of popular children's books. "Very nice. This is much more you."

Marina grinned. "That almost sounds like an insult. This isn't nearly as polished as the look in the other rooms, is it?"

"No, but it's more homey. The other rooms would suit Jillian better than you, I think."

To his surprise, Marina's smile faded and concern shadowed her eyes. "Ben...about Jillian. I love her dearly, but she's a terrible flirt. Please don't take her teasing seriously. She could break your heart without ever meaning to hurt you."

Her words made no sense for the longest time as he turned them over and over in his mind. Finally her meaning penetrated. Slowly, carefully, he asked, "You think I'm attracted to Jillian?"

"I think you could be." She lowered her eyes.

He didn't know whether to laugh or scold her. Didn't she have any inkling of how strongly *she* affected him? "Where did you get that idea?"

She shrugged uncertainly. "You seem to like her. She's a beautiful girl. And you're very vulnerable right now."

"Marina..." Giving in to impulse, he took a step closer and tilted her face up with his index finger. "This is probably a mistake, but I have to show you—I'm not attracted to Jillian." Closing his eyes, he pulled her close and surrendered to the need that had been coiled inside him since the first day he'd seen her standing on her side of the fence.

Six

Marina's mouth was a feast of warmth and softness beneath his. He melded, molded, moistened, angling his head to fit every sweet surface of her lips to his. But Ben only took a moment to appreciate the perfect meshing before delving into her mouth in search of a deeper kiss. She shuddered in his arms when his tongue met hers, and suddenly the cozy little room crackled with too much heat to be contained.

Her hands had been caught between them when he crushed her against him. Now she struggled to free them, sliding her arms up to twine around his neck and pull his head even more closely to hers, spreading her fingers wide to tease the nape of his neck, making him shudder and groan.

She was perfection where their bodies met, so tall

that every inch of her long slim frame met his in a smooth, seamless fit guaranteed to excite and enflame. Her breasts felt small, but they pressed firmly against his chest and he brought a big hand around from her back to boldly palm one pert mound through the fabric of the knit top she wore. When she cried out, he swallowed the erotic sound. Her nails raked his back and she slid them down to clutch his hips as she ground her teeth against his lips in sudden, searing passion, shifting her hips in bold invitation.

Unbearably aroused by her uninhibited response and the feel of her hips undulating against him, Ben bent and slipped an arm under her knees without ever loosening the fit of his mouth over hers. His other arm cradled her back as he swung her into his arms and walked from her den across the hall to the only room she hadn't shown him yet.

Her bedroom.

Part of him absorbed the decor in the dim light from the hallway, the spindled double bed and antique dresser, but he didn't want to think, didn't want to talk. No, he only wanted to feel. Reaching the bed in a few long strides, he let Marina's legs slide down until she was standing before him again. Continuing to kiss her, he savored the sensation of making love to a woman who was nearly as tall as he was, of touching her slender body in all the places he'd wanted to touch.

Her clothes were an impediment now. Almost roughly, he tore at buttons and hooks, then ripped down the zipper on her slacks. Brushing the fabric away from her torso, his hands stilled as he bared her breasts. In a sudden, unexpected motion, Marina turned her head away and even in the darkness he could feel her sudden tensing, sense her embarrassment.

"Don't be shy. I think you're beautiful," he muttered, kissing a bold path from the crest of one taut tip to the other, where he fastened his mouth over the tightly beaded nipple.

When he put his mouth on her breast, she moaned and he caught her weight as her knees buckled. Shifting her backward, he urged her onto the bed.

Her white cat leapt from the bed with one indignant cry and streaked out of the room as their combined weight sank onto the mattress. For uncounted minutes, he lavished attention on her breasts, using his mouth and his fingers until she was moaning and clutching at his back. Finally he lifted his head. Marina lay before him, her shirt flung wide. Her pants were open as well and he could see an enticing triangle of pale skin where he knelt before her.

It wasn't enough. Quickly he stripped the garments away and removed her lacy panties, a deep growl of masculine satisfaction escaping when her lithe, long body lay naked before him. With reverent hands, he stroked from her shoulders down over her fragile rib cage, on to the slight swell of womanly hips and over her outer thighs. The muscles in her calves contracted when he touched them; gently, he went on. Her ankles were so slender his thumb and forefinger met around them, he noted in amazement.

"Such beautiful legs. Do you know how much I've wanted to touch these legs?"

His body was shouting at him to move faster and his pants were rapidly becoming a prison. Still, he didn't rush to remove his own clothing, afraid that without it, his control would be shredded by her small cries and sinuous movements. He took his time tracing a path back up her legs, pausing to feather the lightest of touches over her inner thighs. When she jerked and gasped, he bared his teeth in a smile. "Easy. Take it easy."

Making his way back up her body, he shifted his weight onto her, taking a long moment to simply enjoy the pleasure of lying with her in the beginnings of a mating ritual as old as time. Then he dropped his head to nuzzle at her breasts until he found one budded tip again. He suckled strongly and Marina cried out, digging her heels into the bed and arching her body beneath him.

"Please, Ben, please..." She was almost sobbing. "I need you."

"I know, I know." Her desperation and urgency made him feel more powerful, more masculine, than he'd ever felt before. He let her frantic hands peel his shirt away. "I need you, too."

Rolling to one side, he began to tear at his pants, but she was there before him. His stomach contracted in involuntary delight when she slid her hands inside his waistband; when she inched his zipper down its track, his body leapt and pulsed and he sucked in a harsh breath with a whispered curse that spoke of his tenuous hold on control. He kicked off his shoes and rolled away from her briefly to shuck off his remaining clothes.

When he turned back, the hot, wild meeting of flesh to flesh was more than he could take. "Let me touch you." He slid his hand surely down over her stomach to the nest of fair curls that shielded her woman's center. She parted her legs with no urging, and he moved even farther down to investigate the sweet secrets in the cleft between her legs.

Marina thrashed beneath him, her hands sliding over every inch of his muscled flesh, and he clenched his teeth against a howl of need when a small palm closed over the rigid flesh springing from his groin. She caressed him once, twice, until he tore her hand away, feeling small forerunners of pleasure relentlessly surging through him. Between her thighs, his fingers were slippery with her wet heat. He'd wanted to bring her to pleasure first, to ensure her enjoyment, too, but he could wait no longer.

In some dim corner of his mind, it registered that this woman, this experience, was the most powerfully arousing intimacy he'd ever known. But the thought seemed disloyal and he shied away from further comparisons. Shutting off his mind and going with sensation, he guided himself to the entrance of her body as he took her mouth in a deep, searing kiss again. Wildly she kissed him back, straining against him. "Now, now."

"Yes," he groaned into her mouth. "Now."

He drove himself forward, squeezing his eyes shut

in a grimace of pleasure so great it was almost pain at the tight, hot glide of flesh into flesh. Frantically he tried to reassert a semblance of control but Marina rocked beneath him, increasing the violent rhythms of her hips against his until she was measuring him tip to root with each sweet stroke. He couldn't draw a breath, couldn't form a thought, couldn't stop his own plunging response. When she stiffened and bucked beneath him, shuddering in breaths of gasping completion, he was lost. With a roar of desperation, he succumbed to the need raging through him, pounding into her in a fierce paroxysm of passion that brought him to a jarring, pulsing climax in minutes.

Stunned silence.

For how long? Five, ten minutes?

He lay heavily on her, too winded and lethargic to move. His lips brushed her cheek when he'd dropped to the pillow beside her. Her hands were flattened against his back and she occasionally moved them in small circular caresses that felt incredibly good. Finally, concerned that he was too heavy for her, he raised himself on his arms and withdrew from the chalice of her body, sliding to one side. As he did so, his gaze fell on a framed picture illuminated in the light from the hallway.

He froze, awareness rushing back like an unwelcome winter wind.

Her husband. He'd been a big guy, taller even than Ben himself, and muscled like a bodybuilder, with movie-star blond good looks. Marina was small as a doll snuggled against him.

She'd loved this man. And he was dead.

Just like Carrie.

Carrie. Her image turned his body cold and stiff and any lingering desire shriveled to dust inside him. A sharp-edged knife of grief sliced so deeply that he nearly curled up into a ball and cried out his pain. *Oh, Carrie. I'm sorry. This should have been you.* Memories of holding his wife in the dark, talking and laughing and loving late into the night, marched inexorably through his brain. Guilt rose, so thick he nearly choked as he rolled away from Marina to sit at the edge of the bed with his head in his hands.

"This was a mistake. I'm not ready to say goodbye to Carrie yet."

The silence behind him was total, smothering him in guilt. He wished he were noble enough to reach back and comfort Marina, but he wasn't that selfless. It was taking everything he had in him to face his own loss, his own selfish actions.

His thoughts were racing; barely a moment elapsed between them. Into the hush, she said, "You don't have to say goodbye to Carrie, Ben."

The words made no sense. No matter how he twisted them, he couldn't discern her meaning. At the same time, the hair on the back of his neck prickled in warning. Some instinctive defense mechanism shouted that whatever she was going to say next was something that would affect every corner of his life.

Wanting to deny—what? What? He didn't even know what she was going to say next, but he knew he didn't want to hear it. He repeated, "This was a mistake. I have to leave." Blindly he turned and reached for his clothes.

"Ben!" Marina clutched at him with frantic hands, her fingers digging into his forearm. "Did you hear me? You don't have to lose me. I survived. In this body. *I am Carrie.*"

NO!

Shocked beyond belief at the bizarre words, he threw her off and bolted from the bed. As he turned to grab his clothing, he caught sight of her face.

Marina's hand covered her mouth. Her eyes were huge and her complexion was as white as Jennie's had been when she had the flu. "I didn't plan to tell you." It was a shocked whisper, distorted by the palm over her lips.

His stomach rolled. Automatically his mind rejected her incredible assertion. He didn't believe her, didn't want to believe her, *couldn't believe her!* Through stiff lips, he forced out, "This is an unspeakable, vulgar trick." Rising anger fueled the accusation. "I don't know what kind of horrible people you and your sister are, playing games like this with a grieving person, but let me tell you, I think you're both *sick,* and I'd better not hear either one of you trying to lay this lie on my mother and my daughter—"

"As God is my witness, Ben, *I'm not lying.*" She extended a hand, palm up, as if inviting him to take it, then dropped it when he recoiled. "Please, you can't talk to Jillian, I've never told her...." Tears began to trickle down her cheeks. "It would destroy her to find out that her sister is dead."

He wanted to leave, to run from this place and never look back, to forget he'd ever met a woman named Marina Devereaux.

But he couldn't. *He couldn't.* A note of truth ringing in her voice sent cold chills up and down his spine. *She was lying. She had to be!* All right. So he could play along for now. He'd give her enough rope to hang herself. Grimly he shoved his legs into his pants and yanked them up. As he buttoned and zipped them, he walked to her closet and jerked open the door, grabbing the first robe he saw and flinging it across the room at her. "Get dressed."

"Ben, I—" She tried to put the robe on, but her hands were shaking and the slippery fabric kept sliding out of her grasp. Despite his rage, he felt his loins stir with renewed awareness as her breasts jiggled with her efforts. Furious with himself for being aware of the naked glory of her slim body despite his best efforts to ignore it, he strode back and stuffed her into the robe in a few quick movements, cinching the tie belt so tightly that she squeaked.

"Prove it."

Marina remained where she was, kneeling in the center of the bed with the pale blue robe pooled around her, her bewildered gaze fixed on his face. "I— What?"

"Prove it to me. You have two minutes to convince me that you're serious before I walk out of here."

Her eyes rounded even more. Then, as if someone

had suddenly turned a key, she scrambled off the bed. "All right. Wh-why don't we go into the den and I'll get us some drinks?"

A drink. Yeah. That was the first sensible word out of her mouth since they'd made lo—had sex. "Okay." He stalked across the hall and flopped into the lone recliner, then immediately shot to his feet and began to pace around the room.

She went out to the kitchen and he heard glasses clinking. In a moment, she was back with two snifters and a cookie container. When she handed him his glass, he eyed the contents suspiciously. "What's this?"

She looked up from where she was removing the lid and he was struck by the almost challenging look she threw his way. "Brandy. Our favorite evening drink. And I made some chocolate peanut-butter drops earlier this afternoon, too."

He stared at her. Brandy—and his favorite kind of cookie. The hairs on the back of his neck rose again. *It could be a lucky guess, Bradford.*

Right. And the cookies were just a fluke, even though you don't know another person who's ever made them. Cautiously he picked up a cookie and took a bite, his gaze never leaving hers.

Marina took a deep breath as if fortifying herself for an ordeal. "Major knows me. Jillian's right—the first Marina wasn't an animal lover. She wouldn't know how to train one."

He didn't give her a reaction, although he had to

admit it *was* strange, the way Major obeyed her instantly—just as he'd obeyed Carrie.

When he continued to regard her silently, she offered, "You said I have a lot of Carrie's mannerisms."

"True."

"We met at a dance my freshman year in college. You were a senior. I graduated a semester early and we were married on Valentine's Day. We'll be married six years next February."

That was true, too, but what struck him was the way she referred to them as a couple. "You're not telling me anything that isn't public knowledge."

The challenging look was still in her eye, but her hand shook as she reached for her brandy and absently swirled it—with her left hand, just as Carrie had done. Before he could stop himself, he blurted out, "You're right-handed, aren't you?"

"Ambidextrous," she corrected. Then she took a deep breath and went on. "We went on a cruise to St. Thomas on our honeymoon. The following year, we took another cruise because we'd enjoyed the first one so much, but there was one big difference."

He waited.

"Before we left, you gave me a little box that contained several kinds of oil. We missed dinner the first night out experimenting, and we spent most of the rest of the trip in our stateroom. Your mother couldn't understand it when I came back without a tan."

Ben felt goose bumps rise all over his arms. "What

happened the night I gave you your engagement ring?''

''I cried and accepted your proposal. I'd been resisting your attempts to take me to bed, because it was important to me to wait for the man I married. But after you proposed, I realized I loved you enough to want you to be the first, even if our plans fell apart.'' She smiled ruefully and focused her intense blue gaze on his face. ''And when I asked you to make love to me—you refused because you said I was worth waiting for.''

The silence was pregnant with tension. Ben could hear his own breath rasping in and out of his lungs. ''What names did we have picked out for our first child and why did we name her Jennie?''

''For a boy, we'd chosen Daniel Blayne, after your mother's maiden name. A girl was supposed to be Emily Diane, but on the way into the hospital when I was in labor we heard a man calling his dog Jennie and you said, 'Jennie's cute. I like that a hell of a lot better than Emily.'''

''What were we talking about on the way to the park the day you were—hit?''

Marina's eyes filled with tears. ''We weren't talking. We hadn't talked much at all since I had my tubes tied. The doctor recommended it after I had such a difficult time with Jennie, but it was so hard for us to accept that we waited another eighteen months, until we had a scare when I thought I was pregnant. The doctor reminded you that an accidental pregnancy could kill me. I had a tubal ligation the following week." A sob escaped and she bowed her head, her intertwined fingers clasped so tightly the knuckles were white. "I know you've always wanted a big family. I was afraid you didn't love me anymore."

He covered his face, and his muffled voice was poignant with the anguish he felt. "*This can't be. How can you know all these things?*" The question reflected all the confusion, all the fear and uncertainty rolling through him, scattering his firmly grounded concepts of death and a hereafter.

Abruptly he straightened, backing away when she would have come toward him. "I have to leave. I—I have to think." He felt as if his brain were shutting down, slowly being deprived of oxygen. None of the information she'd just thrown at him was being assimilated; it was all floating around in his mind like isolated letters in a bowl of alphabet soup.

Pivoting without another word, he strode down the hallway and grabbed his jacket off the back of a kitchen chair, not stopping to shrug into it until he had the door open and was outside, breathing the fresh, bitingly cold winter air. He was acting irrationally, knew he was being insensitive, but in this situation, he figured he was entitled. He had to get away from her until he could think things through.

Things. He shook his head, aware that his pulse was pounding as though he'd run a five-minute mile. *What the hell was the protocol to follow when a woman tells you she's your wife returned from the dead?*

* * *

Marina was at the shop early the next morning. She hadn't slept at all after the disaster the previous evening.

He didn't believe me. Tears filled her eyes again. She'd cried so much last night she'd been sure there was not one drop of moisture left within her.

She'd never intended to tell him at all. But after the cataclysmic lovemaking that she sensed had been as far out of his control as it had hers, the words had just…said themselves.

This is all my fault, she reminded herself. *I got a second chance. I should have gone away, started my life in some new place, never tried to see Ben or Jennie again. Now I've ruined everything I've built since July.*

Compounding her misery was the fear that Ben would make good on his threat to confront Jillian with the story. The mere idea brought more tears. Pulling a crumpled, well-used tissue from the pocket of her corduroy jumper, she wiped her eyes and began the process of opening up the cash register.

"'Morning! Ready to work until we drop?" Jillian shucked off a stylish winter dress coat as she breezed through the door.

"Yeah." Marina's face was subdued. She knew her sister was referring to the fact that the Friday after Thanksgiving was traditionally the biggest shopping day of the year.

Jillian walked around to the front of the register and peered at Marina. "Such enthusiasm. You feel okay?" The concern in her voice increased to alarm as she got a glimpse of Marina's puffy eyes. "What's wrong?"

Marina sniffled. "Nothing. Just something I have to work out on my own."

Jillian's eyes narrowed. "Does this involve a certain charming widower who could hardly wait until I left last night to be alone with you?"

Marina bit her lip and nodded.

"I'll string him up and gut him with a broken pencil if he hurt you. What happened?"

"Jillian!" Marina had to smile at the bloodthirsty tone and graphic imagery. Her sister's instant defense lifted the cloud of misery a fraction. "It wasn't his fault. We just had a...a misunderstanding."

"A misunderstanding."

"Uh-huh. Trust me. I'll be okay."

"If you say so." Jillian heaved a sigh. "Why do we do this to ourselves? Men are nothing but misery."

"That's not strictly true." Marina wondered what had happened in Jillian's life to produce the pain she saw in her sister's eyes.

"Yes, it is." Jill's voice was certain, with an underlying note of bitterness. "We're brought up to believe in fairy tales. Every little girl will find her Prince Charming and live happily ever after and all that garbage."

Marina thought of how happy Carrie had been with Ben until the trouble over childbearing entered their lives. "Sometimes it happens."

"Not often. Most of the time, reality slaps us in

the face and we find our Prince Charming is a frog no amount of kissing can improve.''

Forgetting her own troubles for the moment, Marina reached over the counter and grasped Jillian's hand. ''Is that what happened to you?''

Jillian's gaze searched Marina's for a moment. ''Sometimes I can't *believe* you don't remember *anything*.'' Then she shrugged. ''In this case, it's just as well. That part of my life is something I only want to forget.''

In some small way, it was important to Marina to realize that someone in this new world she'd entered needed her, that she wasn't the only one harboring secret hurts. Squeezing her sister's hand, she said, ''If you ever want to talk, I'm a good sounding board.''

Jillian shook her head, and Marina could almost see her shrugging off the momentary mood. ''Why don't we agree to forget that men exist?''

The day was every bit as hectic as they'd anticipated and Marina was grateful that she didn't have time to think. Driving home late that night, her feet hurt, her back ached and her mind was foggy with figures from all the sales she'd made. And yet, her thoughts had returned to Ben every free second she'd found throughout the day. The minute she entered the house, she changed into her most comfortable sweat suit and headed for the kitchen.

She was just devouring the last bite of a cold supper when the doorbell rang. Her heart leapt as high as both of her pets at the sound. *It's probably only Jill,* she admonished herself. *No one else has any rea-*

son to be ringing your bell at this hour. Deliberately she refused to let herself think of Ben.

But when she flipped on the outside light, it *was* Ben she saw standing on the stoop. His hair was rumpled and he looked as haggard as she felt; still, her body quickened at the memory of the physical intimacies they'd shared last night. Her fingers fumbled with the locks as she opened the door.

"Let's say, just for the sake of harmony, that I believe you." Ben exhaled deeply, not even bothering with a greeting. "Explain it to me...what, how...."

She was careful not to let the joy bounding through her show as she invited him in. *He didn't say he believes you. Don't get excited. And anyway, even if he does believe you, that doesn't mean you two can continue to be...friends. Things have changed too much.*

He accepted her offer of a drink. When they were seated in her den, there was an expectant silence. Finally she asked, "Where do you want me to start?"

"From the beginning. From the accident, if you can."

She was glad she didn't have to talk about that. She could see the dread those memories still evoked in him. "I don't remember the accident. I have a vague memory of hurting, and people talking, but the first thing that's clear in my mind is when I watched the trauma team working on this dark-haired girl who was obviously in bad shape—and I realized it was me."

Ben's expression told her how hard it was for him to think about her injuries. But his voice was strong as he queried, "Watching? Where were you watching from?"

She told him everything she could, searching desperately for human terms to describe what was beyond the limits of human vocabulary to convey. Several times he stopped her, but for the most part, he simply listened as she described seeing him in the waiting room and how she'd gone to the Place of Light.

She made an effort to be as accurate as possible, but when she came to the meeting with the dual being that she now believed to be Ron and the first Marina, she paraphrased the statements that she still remembered perfectly, unwilling to imply that she and Ben might have a future together. *Someday you'll understand—you and Ben.*

When she finished, she couldn't tell what he was thinking from the shuttered expression on his handsome face. Sprawled on her sofa, he swirled his drink and stared off into space for so long that she couldn't stand it anymore. "Well?"

"Well what?"

"Do you believe me?"

"It's a lot to digest," he said, evading her question. "I don't know much about out-of-body experiences, or the near-death stuff or reincarnation, but what you tell me is consistent with what little I've read."

She stood in agitation and went to the single window to stare into the black night beyond. "I've read everything I could find since...since July. Apparently these kinds of experiences have been happening to people for a long, long time. But I'm one of very few who claim to have come back in another body *in the same lifetime.*"

"There are others?" Ben sat forward.

Marina spun from the window. "Not living. And none whose documentation approaches the experience I've had." She gestured wildly with her hands. "But that doesn't mean there aren't more out there. Why would anyone choose to destroy their anonymity by telling a crazy story like this? I'd be laughed at, harassed—a freak and a crazy kind of celebrity for the rest of my life." She laughed, but it was a sound of despair. "Or whoever's life this is now."

Seven

The silence in Marina's den was oppressive, uncomfortable. Ben slumped against the back of the couch, staring at a print on the wall without even seeing it. His thoughts were whirling, careering wildly through his mind as they'd been since she'd blurted out her first unbelievable words last night.

God, had it only been last night? Only twenty-four short hours ago? He felt ages older, as if he'd survived a war or some devastating natural disaster like an earthquake. He couldn't remember a thing he'd done at work today. He'd called his mother to ask if she could keep Jennie overnight, telling her something unexpected had cropped up, but he couldn't even recall what she'd replied. Since he was here, she must have agreed.

"What do you want from me?" He hadn't meant it to come out so baldly. Vaguely he regretted the aggressive tone he'd used, but he might as well get it out in the open. This was the crux of the matter—assuming he believed her, which he was beginning to do, regardless of how crazy her tale seemed. As far as he could figure, there was absolutely no way anyone could have gleaned all the hidden details of his life with Carrie that Marina possessed.

Unwillingly he reviewed all the times he'd been taken aback by small things that had reminded him of his wife...the way Marina used "sugar" as pseudo-curse, her love of animals, the way she could make even the deadest-looking plant grow, her dislike of pumpkin pie, her vigilant campaign against junk food, her cooking.

In the few weeks he'd known her, she'd managed to make nearly all of his favorite foods without being asked. She wiped down the kitchen like she was attacking a mortal enemy after every meal. Even the way she crossed her arms defensively when they disagreed was familiar, as was the way she caught the tip of her tongue between her teeth when she watered the plants. He hadn't seen the yellow watering pitcher that Carrie had used since she died, but Marina had found it and used it the first time she was left alone in his kitchen. And here in her home, her books were shelved alphabetically by author, just as Carrie had always done. The towels in her bathroom were folded in the same unusual fancy manner and he'd been floored to find that she drank the same special brand of decaf tea that Carrie had—with exactly a quarter of a pack of sweetener added.

Taken separately, all those things were no more than coincidence. Millions of other people around the world probably shared any of those particular quirks. But *all* of them? Added together, the ways in which Marina resembled Carrie were distinctly spooky. Combined with the secrets she knew about their life together, he couldn't imagine how she could have fabricated it.

But then—that meant she *was* Carrie. Shouldn't he want her back? Did he?

Marina looked shocked at his question. Her eyes were shiny again, as if she was holding back tears. She'd looked like that all evening. "I don't want anything from you." Her voice was low, almost defeated, but firm. "I didn't plan to come here, to disrupt your life. When I saw this house for sale, I made an impulse decision. I only wanted to be near enough to see you and Jennie from time to time."

Her voice grew in volume and rose steadily higher; he was appalled to see the tears he'd detected begin to cascade down her cheeks. "Do you think I wanted this? Do you think I *chose* to come back to a life in which I lost every single thing that was familiar? To know my baby is growing up just a few yards away and I'm missing all those precious moments? To live every day knowing that eventually you'll fall in love with someone else and remarry? I only resisted leaving because I wanted to reassure you, to let you know that I'd be waiting—that we'd be together again someday. I didn't plan to stay for good. If I'd had any idea about the loneliness..." She paused and seared him with a look that contained all the anguish she'd felt since she'd awakened in the hospital as Marina Devereaux. "I'd have gone," she finished bitterly. "I wouldn't have fought so hard to come back."

"Marina—"

"No!" Weeping openly, she turned from him, gesturing with one hand toward the door. "Go, Ben. There's no point in dragging this out any further."

He should. He should forget this whole impossible mess, go home and get on with what was left of his life. But...

His life was here in this room.

Even before Marina had told him about coming back, he'd been more attracted to her than he'd ever been to any other woman besides his wife. He'd been picking up the pieces of his life that were shattered when Carrie died and slowly gluing them back into a serviceable whole when Marina came along. She'd speeded up the process, given him something to look forward to, moments of sweetness, shared laughter and a closeness he'd feared he'd lost forever.

And no wonder. Something inside him had sensed her familiarity, even if his conscious mind hadn't allowed him to consider it at first.

Rising from the sofa, he stepped toward her and placed his hands on her shoulders. She went rigid under his hands for an instant, then flung herself into his arms, sobbing.

Closing his arms around her, he buried his face in her hair. Without a conscious decision, his heart accepted what his mind was reluctant to believe.

"Welcome home, my love."

The next day was Saturday. Ben had asked her to spend the day with him and Jennie, and Marina was awake just after dawn, savoring the anticipation.

Ben had stayed last night, though they'd talked into the wee hours. In a way, she was glad. Their relationship felt fragile, new and untried, and she wasn't ready for more intimacy of a physical nature. Exciting as it had been, the mad loving they'd shared had spawned new insecurities. This body was very different from Carrie's. She had no breasts to speak of now, a fact that dismayed her almost as much as her long legs and slim hips delighted her. And she hated her hair—short and flyaway. There was no way she could let it grow into the thick, waving mass of heavy curls that Carrie had possessed. That Ben had loved to play with and Jennie had clutched in one tiny fist while she nursed as an infant.

And that wasn't the worst of it. In addition to her fears that Ben wouldn't like this body, she almost resented the fact that he appeared to be madly attracted to her. It felt like he was cheating on her…or on Carrie. But how could he be when she was herself?

It was too exhausting to contemplate. All she did was go in mental circles with that line of thinking. It made her more sure than ever that they shouldn't jump right back into a physical relationship until they'd had a chance to get to know each other again.

And yet her body had practically whimpered aloud when he'd hugged her and gone home alone last night.

She'd showered and dressed and was contemplating breakfast when a knock at the back door sent Lucky into a frenzy of barking. Her pulse doubled as she hurried to unlock the door, already sure it was Ben.

He stood on the stoop, smiling at her, his hair still gleaming with moisture from his shower. As always, her heart skipped a beat at the sight of his dark good looks. His green eyes matched the green of his sweatshirt; they shone with a private warmth, although he didn't touch her. "Good morning."

She wondered if her grin looked as slaphappy as she felt. "Good morning. Come on in." She glanced at the wall clock above the sink. "Do you realize it's only seven-thirty?"

"Yep." He looked sheepish. "I came across the backyard so the neighbors wouldn't see me."

"Wise move."

"I can think of a better one." He strode purposefully across the kitchen.

She'd retreated a few feet when he stepped into the doorway, more because he was so big than from any real unease. But the gleam in his eye had her stumbling backward until she came up against the counter by the sink. "Ben, uh, I've been thinking—"

"Me, too. All night long. Let me tell you what I

thought about.'' He gripped the counter on either side
of her and slowly, deliberately, leaned his body closer
until her legs were forced to separate to admit his
thighs between them. The heat of his chest fired
awareness through the fabric of her cotton blouse.
When his thighs rested flush against the sensitive feminine flesh at the V of her legs and his mouth moved
warmly against her ear, she was swamped by sensation. The graphic words he growled brought a blush
to her cheeks, but as he nibbled at the vulnerable skin
below her ear, she shuddered and all coherent thought
fled.

''Stop. Ah, I, ah, we…'' His mouth brushed across
her cheek and she grasped all her willpower in both
hands as she seized handfuls of his thick hair and
pulled his head away. ''Ben, wait!''

His eyes were alight with amusement and desire.
''I've been waiting all night.''

She wanted him too much to resist when he pulled
her more firmly against him and lowered his head to
find her mouth. As he invaded her mouth with insistent strokes of his tongue that demanded response, she
was engulfed in an inferno of need, ablaze with sweet,
shaking sensation that tightened her nipples almost
painfully and pulled taut strings of desire even tighter
in her abdomen. The hot strength of man she could
feel pushing at her was a potent inducement to let
him work his sensual magic, to simply slide down to
the floor and open herself to the raging rush of fulfillment her body craved.

But it wasn't her body. And more important, it wasn't *her* body Ben wanted.

The thought was an unwelcome dash of ice water on the flames that consumed her. Tearing her mouth from his, she buried her head in his shoulder. "Ben—stop. This is too soon." She gasped for breath as he transferred his attention to the rim of her ear. "I don't feel comfortable with this yet." Emotionally, that was true; physically, it was a lie of the greatest magnitude.

His mouth stilled and his hands relaxed their insistent stroking. "I wouldn't describe what I'm feeling as comfortable, but I don't want to stop." But his tone was wry and she sensed that she'd gotten through. He dropped a kiss on her forehead and rocked his hips against her once more before levering himself away. "I'm sorry. I know we need time. I decided last night that I needed to treat this like a normal courtship as much as possible—to give us time to adjust to being together again."

Her eyes filled as the sincerity in his tone registered and her throat closed up so quickly she couldn't reply.

He gave her a lopsided smile and took her hand, carefully lacing her fingers through his. "Want to go to Mom's with me to pick up Jennie?"

"I'd love to, but...it's pretty early. Have you eaten?"

He turned interested eyes on her. "Nope. You offering to cook?"

"Blueberry pancakes."

He rolled his eyes skyward. "Hog heaven! I

haven't had blueberry pancakes since—'' He stopped abruptly.

"Since the accident." Her voice was low.

"Damn." He slammed a fist down on the counter. "How do we get around this? Everything I say or do reminds me—and you—of our life before. We have to start fresh."

"I know." She met his eyes squarely. "Carrie Bradford is dead. I am Marina Devereaux now. It's difficult, but it will get easier with practice." She almost choked on the words. In some ways, she was having more trouble being Marina now than she had since she woke up in the hospital.

Ben spread his hands in frustration. "I'll do my best to stay in the present."

"I don't mind if we talk about Carrie sometimes." She didn't think it would be healthy for either of them to ignore the unusual circumstances of their new relationship. As she took out a mixing bowl, she hesitated. "There is something else we should discuss."

"What's that?" Ben was watching her closely.

"I need to know what you intend to do with the knowledge of the experience I've shared with you." She pointed a wooden spoon at him.

"That depends on you."

"On me?"

"Yeah. Personally, I would rather you didn't tell anyone else. I think the publicity that would result from coming forward with an incredible story like this would totally disrupt any chance we have at a normal family life. I think it could be harmful to Jennie.

But..." he held up a palm as she opened her mouth "...if it's important to you to share this with the world, then I'll support your decision and I promise you I'll do everything I can to minimize the impact on our lives."

Marina nodded slowly. "Thank you." It wasn't all she wanted to say, but she didn't trust herself to go any further. Then she realized Ben was waiting for her to state her feelings on the matter. "I—I'd rather we didn't share this with anyone, either. It's almost too incredible to be believed. Sometimes *I* have a hard time believing it. I do wonder if there's anyone else out there struggling with...coming back...but all I wanted when I realized I was Marina was to live quietly and maybe see you and Jennie from a distance occasionally. Now—" She paused, not wanting to take too much for granted. "Now I already feel as if I've been luckier than I can believe. I'm just going to take one day at a time."

He nodded. "Sounds good to me. There are a few things we'll need to plan, but for the most part, I agree."

"What will we need to plan?"

"Our wedding, for one thing." He frowned. "Combining two households is going to take some work. We can get married quietly without raising too many eyebrows—maybe right after Christmas?—but I'm not waiting much longer than that."

Once again, her throat closed up. She'd been afraid to consider the long-term implications of this new situation, afraid to even hope that he would want to invite her back into his life. "You want to get married?"

"Of course I want to get married." He stepped closer and grasped her elbows, smiling tenderly. "We already *are* married, but for Jennie's sake we'll have to be conventional. You're technically a widow, remember?"

"I know. I just hadn't expected... I wasn't sure—"

He grimaced. "I'm sorry I was so rough on you at first. I couldn't imagine, but I do believe you."

"I don't blame you." She stroked his morning-smooth jaw with a gentle palm. "It does sound crazy."

He turned his mouth into her cupped hand. "You still haven't given me an answer."

She shivered as his tongue traced her palm. "Um, what was the question?"

"Marriage, woman." He took her hands between both of his larger ones and regarded her soberly. "Marina Devereaux, will you marry me?"

The tears wouldn't be denied. She smiled through them as she allowed her heart to shine in her gaze. "I'd be honored."

Sunday was mild and Ben drove them to the Baltimore Zoo. He was oddly touched when Marina complimented him on Jennie's development since the summer.

"She's surprisingly secure for a child who lost her mother. You must have worked hard to overcome that."

He nodded his head slowly. "According to the psychologist I've been consulting, she's doing reasonably well. It hasn't been easy, but having my mother near has helped give Jennie a sense of stability. Mom's devoted herself to us since July."

Marina squeezed his hand as they watched Jennie giggle at the antics of the two polar bears. "I'll always be grateful to Helen, even though I can't tell her."

As they turned from the polar bears to go in search of a drink, he spotted a couple from his church who had children a few years older than Jennie. They were staring openly at Marina and the easy way in which he clasped her hand as they walked along. He smiled and waved.

"Don't look now," he said, "but Ken and June Larrier are here. They look slightly astounded to see me holding hands with a beautiful blonde."

"June Larrier's an awful gossip." Marina sighed. "The whole church will know by next Sunday. You'll probably get some well-meant advice and a lecture or two on not rushing into anything too soon after your wife's death."

"I'll tell them my wife gave me express permission to rush into something with this particular lady." Ben felt his body tighten when Marina flashed him a dimpled smile. Although logically he knew it would be a bad move to establish physical intimacy again without taking time to overcome the constraints he felt between them after the separation, his body was urging him to take her back to bed. Every move she made reminded him in some way of the uninhibited passion in her response to him only three nights ago.

To get his mind off the intensity of his physical discomfort, he suggested, "Why don't you attend church with us next Sunday? I can introduce you and then the pastor won't be so shocked when we call him to talk about the wedding."

Marina looked thoughtful. "That's a good idea. But it's going to seem funny meeting people I already know."

"I know." Sometimes he was as overwhelmed by the strangeness of this whole experience as she clearly was. He couldn't imagine how she'd handled it alone for five months. She hadn't even told Jillian, who was now her sister and had become one of her closest friends. Apparently his little Carrie had been made of stronger stuff than he'd realized.

They had dinner together every night during the following week. On Thursday evening, after Marina had bathed Jennie, read a story and tucked her into bed, she joined him on the sofa in the family room.

With one arm comfortably around Marina, he flipped through the television schedule. He was about to press the remote button to turn on the television, when she said, "Ben?"

Her voice was strangely hesitant and his chest tightened. The only time he'd heard that tone in her voice were the times when they'd discussed the painful details of their life together...before. He found himself giving the phrase Marina's inflection.

"What?"

"Would it bother you if we watched some of our home movies tonight?"

He didn't know what he'd expected her to say, but that wasn't it. He realized he'd been holding his breath, fearing what her serious tone preceded. Relief made him giddy. "Not at all. I have a few you've never seen that have been taken since July."

When he'd set up the recorder to show the movies, he returned to her side. "Where do you want to start?"

"I don't care." Her voice was subdued. He squeezed her shoulder gently. The feel of her soft flesh under his palm was a subtle arousal, but he shunted his body's response aside. He'd been giving her all the room she seemed to need, doing his damnedest to be affectionate without pressing her for passion. It was hard when his body perked up at the merest whiff of her scent, the tiniest whisper of her voice, the lightest brush of her slender form against his.

Damn hard, he thought, shifting slightly to relieve the pressure in his jeans.

The first pictures they saw were of Jennie in last year's Easter finery, toddling through the yard with a basket nearly as big as she was. Each time she discovered an egg, she squealed with joy. After she found the third egg, the basket began to get heavy and Carrie appeared in the frames, taking the basket and directing Jennie to a flower bed where more decorated eggs waited. Carrie's Easter dress was an adult version of Jennie's, but the delicate fabric swelled over her full breasts. When his mother walked into view, he was shocked to see how much taller she was than his wife. He'd forgotten how short Carrie was.

He studied the film intently. How did he feel? How was he supposed to feel? The familiar longing welled up in him along with a bittersweet sadness. He still missed her. Not *her,* so much as her familiar form, her eyes, her face....

He was beginning to accept that he still had his wife, that he hadn't lost the companionship, the heart and soul of the woman he'd loved. But it was all so crazy. Why had this happened? Why couldn't he just have Carrie back? Why couldn't everything be like it had been before the accident?

Carrie had been given a second chance—by God, or whatever all-powerful being had orchestrated her return. If He was so capable, why hadn't He simply returned her in her original shell? Why the switch?

Maybe it was some kind of grand joke on him. Or a test. Hell, he'd failed miserably if that was the case. He'd known Marina for less than six weeks when he took her to bed—and he hadn't known she was Carrie when he'd done it.

Guilt surfaced from deep down where it had been hiding, a living presence gnawing at his gut. He'd been attracted to Marina from the first day they'd met and he'd acted on it practically the first time they'd been truly alone together. He wondered what she thought of the haste with which he'd forsaken celibacy. Uncomfortably he glanced over at her, deciding she would be justified in being angry at his attraction to another woman mere weeks after she'd died.

Her face was pale and she was biting her lip. Her hands, usually so graceful with their long, slender fingers, were clenched tightly together. He could see angry red crescents on the backs of her hands where her nails were digging in, and her knuckles were white. Shaken out of his own dark thoughts, he angled his body toward her where she sat beside him on the couch.

"Marina?"

She tore her gaze away from the screen and looked at him and he nearly flinched from the sorrow in the depths of her blue eyes.

"I feel as if someone very close to me has died." Her voice was so low he had to strain to make out the words. "Seeing myself—you can't fathom what it's like to look in the mirror and see a stranger's face every morning."

The shaking despair in her voice confounded him. Striving for a comforting tone, he said, "No, I can't. But your new face and figure are very attractive—"

"But I don't *want* a new face and figure," she said fiercely. "I just want my old one back." Then she turned away from him. "Unlike you."

"What's that supposed to mean?" Her sudden attack caught him squarely in his most vulnerable spot as her words mirrored his very thoughts.

"You don't seem to be too devastated at the loss of the old me." She was still staring at the far wall, but there was no mistaking the hurt in her sarcastic tone.

He didn't know what to say. Carrie had never attacked him in such a fashion. Slowly he reached over and took her hands in his, smoothing his thumbs over the marks her nails had made.

"Ah, honey, I wish we could go back to the way we were, too. I wish the past six months could be erased from our lives. But they can't." He lifted her hands and kissed the damaged flesh of each one in turn. "It's true. I am attracted to this body. There's no excuse for my behavior before I knew who you were and I can't blame you for resenting that. But think about this—I believe that without your unique personality inside this body, it would have held no special appeal for me. I was so attracted precisely because you have all the Carrie qualities that I love."

Her eyebrows rose and her forehead wrinkled in thought. He was heartened. At least she wasn't shutting him out.

Sliding his palms along her arms to her shoulders, he said, "Don't ever make the mistake of thinking I don't miss Carrie. If I could look over and see that familiar smile, those eyes..." He sighed. "But that doesn't mean I'll love you any less in this body, either. I know that doesn't make any sense. It barely makes sense to me. Like you said, it's an impossible situation. All we can do is give it time."

When he'd finished voicing his jumbled thoughts, there was a long silence in the room. He continued to stroke her shoulders, finding a small relief in the fact that she hadn't pulled away from his touch.

Then she offered him a tentative smile and his heart rose like a hot-air balloon as he read the love in her gaze. ''I'm sorry for taking that cheap shot at you a minute ago.'' She leaned her forehead trustingly against his and he wrapped his arms around her, loving the way her arms came up as he bent his head and buried it in her neck. There was nothing sexual in the embrace, but he didn't care. Comfort was far more important.

On Saturday, Marina suggested that Ben bring Jennie down to the store after her nap. Jillian had coerced a friend's husband into dressing up as Santa and sitting in the store for a few hours. Marina wanted Jennie to sit on Santa's lap. They'd been talking about it all week and Jennie couldn't wait to get her first glimpse of Santa Claus.

When they arrived, Kids' Place was teeming with parents and active offspring. Ben had barely gotten Jennie's coat off when she burst into tears and reached her arms up to be held. He couldn't blame her. The shop was a madhouse. For someone who wasn't even three feet tall, it must be incredibly frightening. Rubbing Jennie's back, he carried her through the throng to where he spotted a blond head.

But it was Jill he'd found. Disappointment and irritation sharpened his voice. ''Where's Marina?''

Jillian cast him a beleaguered smile. ''She's

Santa's helper for a while. Go on over and elbow your way to the front. I know she's been looking for you.''

Turning in the direction she pointed, he saw Marina, wearing a red hat with a white ball on the tail that dropped down over one ear. She should have looked ridiculous, but somehow she managed to look incredibly appealing.

Just then, she glanced up and saw him. A smile lit her face, transforming her from simply pretty to one of the most gorgeous women he'd ever laid eyes on. He was caught off guard by a blast of desire that slammed into him like a freight train. It wasn't a feeling he was used to, and he wasn't sure he liked it. Carrie had been sexy in her own sloe-eyed, quiet way, but she hadn't been a head turner like this. He'd be fighting off other men for the rest of his life.

People around her had turned to look when she smiled and waved, and he started forward. Jennie had her face buried in his jacket and he whispered in her ear, "Look, Jen. There's Marina and Santa.''

Jennie raised her face a fraction. When her seeking gaze found Marina, she lunged out of his arms. Marina rushed forward and caught her with the lightning-quick reflexes of a true mother, laughing and tickling her tummy.

"Hi, baby. Look who came to see me today. Would you like to sit on Santa's lap and tell him what you want for Christmas?''

Jennie solemnly regarded Santa, who winked at her and patted his knee. "No. 'Tay wif you.''

"Santa has a special treat for little girls who sit on his lap," Marina cajoled.

Jennie shook her head and clutched Marina tighter.

"Maybe she's too young," Ben suggested. "Next year she might not be so frightened."

But Marina wasn't giving up. "I haven't talked to Santa yet. How about if I sit on his lap and you sit on my lap while I talk to Santa?"

Jennie thought for a moment, then nodded. "Otay."

Grinning triumphantly, Marina stepped toward the red-suited man seated in a sturdy chair. As she seated herself on his knees with Jennie clinging tightly to her neck, Ben was momentarily distracted by a twinge of envy. If only she were sitting on *his* knees—he'd like to have that heart-shaped bottom snuggling onto his lap.

Annoyed by the surge of sexual excitement the thought produced, he focused all his attention on his daughter and his…wife. To-be. He noted that Santa had the good sense to speak in a quiet, reassuring tone to Jennie. If he'd boomed, "Ho-ho-ho," Ben could have predicted Jennie's reaction. Tears. With a capital *T*, probably accompanied by a healthy scream or six.

As Marina comforted her, Jennie managed to mumble a few phrases in the general direction of the jolly old elf. But when Santa offered her a red-and-white striped candy cane, she abandoned her shy pose and shouted, "Look, Daddy! San'a gived me can-dee!"

As Ben smiled and nodded, the part-time girl who was helping during the Christmas season grasped his elbow and urged him toward the chair. "Go up there and kneel beside Santa's chair. I'll take a picture of all of you."

"No, that's—"

"Come on, Ben. It's the first time Jennie ever talked to Santa. We need a picture to remember this occasion." Marina beckoned to him with a smile.

Acceding, he knelt at Santa's side, behind the knee on which Marina sat. As the girl focused on the shot, he sneaked one hand forward and rested it on Marina's thigh. Marina's warm, firm thigh. When the picture was taken, he rose, taking Jennie from Marina. "Walk out front with me," he commanded.

She looked up at him, and the love shining in her wide blue eyes warmed him all the way down to his toes. "All right."

As they eased their way through the crowd, a gray-haired woman patted Jennie on the arm. "Your daughter is adorable," she said to Marina.

Marina beamed, but she shook her head. "She isn't mine."

"But she soon will be." He didn't know what had possessed him to say it, but he saw Marina stiffen as if she wasn't pleased. The woman moved away, and suddenly he realized why Marina had reacted as she did. Jillian stood directly in front of them.

Her eyes were wide and she looked rather shocked. "Did I hear you right?" she demanded of him.

"Depends on what you heard."

She shook her finger under his nose. "Don't get

smart with me, buddy. Are you going to marry my sister?''

He laughed at her ferocious expression as he grabbed Jill's shoulders and planted a quick, exuberant kiss on her lips. ''Yeah. You got something to say about it?''

She looked slightly dazed as she pressed her fingers to her lips. Then her eyes focused and she turned to Marina. ''Good luck. You're going to need it to keep this one in line.'' And before Marina could respond, Jill dashed away to help a customer.

Ben was amused. ''Does anything ever throw her off balance for long?''

''I'm not sure. A man once, maybe.'' Marina's answer was slow, her tone almost cool as she bent and set Jennie down.

His eyes narrowed. What the hell was wrong now? ''Is there a problem?''

''No.''

''Then why do I feel as if you're a dog and I'm a flea you'd like to scratch right off?''

She didn't even crack a smile. ''You caught me off guard when you announced our plans to my only living relative. I'm trying to figure out how to deal with the questions I know she's going to throw at me the minute you walk out that door.''

''I'm sorry.'' He meant it. He wasn't used to sharing Car—Marina with anyone.

''I guess I hadn't expected to tell anybody quite yet. It doesn't matter.'' But she wouldn't meet his eyes.

"Will I see you tonight?" He felt as if she'd thrown up a wall between them and he wasn't sure why. It seemed vital that he get to the bottom of the problem.

She nodded. "I'll come over as soon as I feed the animals and change."

"All right. I'll save you some dinner."

"Thanks." She glanced around in a distracted manner. "I have to get back to work. We're swamped today. Jill's promotion on the Santa visit brought in more business than we'd dreamed."

"This is something I won't miss when we're married." He surveyed the crowded shop with mild distaste. This damned business took up far too much of her time and attention to suit him. "It'll be nice to have you home again."

Eight

After Jennie was in bed, Marina sat with Ben on the couch. The silence seemed strained and she sought for a neutral topic to discuss. Why hadn't she responded more enthusiastically when Ben had told Jillian about their wedding plans that afternoon? Why had it bothered her so much?

She loved him. Having another opportunity to spend her life with him was more than she'd ever dreamed she could have. And she wanted it more than anything else in the world.

And yet, there was a flaw in the fabric of her happiness that she was just beginning to notice. Had Ben always been so...autocratic? Was autocratic even the right word? He loved her, he'd always been thoughtful and considerate of her wishes—but had she had any ideas that weren't molded by him?

It obviously hadn't occurred to him that she might want to break the news of their plans to Jillian herself. Just as he clearly hadn't considered that she might want to continue her work at the store after they married.

He'd always wanted a wife who would stay at home. She'd understood his need to build a solid family framework after the trauma of his early years. Losing his father and then watching his mother work two jobs to make ends meet had made a lasting impression. He was determined that his wife would never have to work, seemed to need to prove that he could provide for her. And she'd been happy to comply. She'd loved cooking and homemaking, and after Jennie was born she'd felt completely and utterly fulfilled.

But she was different now, in ways that went far deeper than the physical changes she'd undergone. She no longer felt satisfied staying at home all the time. Even loving Jennie as much as she did, she knew she'd go crazy if she didn't get into the store on a regular basis.

The store. When Jillian had dragged her into Kids' Place that first time, she'd been terrified. Carrie Bradford had never had any experiences that prepared her for suddenly owning half of a thriving enterprise. She'd been surprised to realize that she enjoyed learning all the ins and outs of the business as Jillian patiently taught her everything the old Marina had known and done.

It would kill her to give it up.

Let's not exaggerate, Marina.

Well, okay, it might not kill her, but she wouldn't be happy any longer as an at-home mom. Besides, with the kind of shop she owned, Jennie could even accompany her some of the time. The best of both worlds.

So why didn't she think Ben would see it like that?

Ben flipped on the television to a news program before the silence between them grew uncomfortable. Even as confused as she was, when he put his arm around her and his long thigh brushed hers as he snuggled her close, she felt a twinge of pleasurable arousal that faded to a warm glow when he made no further demands.

When the program ended, she stood reluctantly. The heat of Ben's body and his comforting nearness had almost convinced her to shut her eyes and drift off to sleep. "I've had a big day. I'd better call it a night."

Ben stood, too. Before she could move, he lifted his arms and slid them loosely around her waist, pulling her to him. "I can't wait until we can live in the same house again. This is driving me crazy, having to let you go every night."

"I know." In the low heels she wore to work, she could nearly look him in the eye. She dropped her head to his shoulder, wanting to be cuddled and comforted, but the position was uncomfortable. Abruptly she was overwhelmed by it all—all the changes her life had undergone. She felt as if she and Ben weren't going to agree on anything ever again. She sensed that he was still struggling with her new identity at some level. Did he believe her? And to top it off, this new body was so very *different.*

She jerked her head off his shoulder and pulled away from his arms, shaking her head bitterly. "Nothing's the same anymore. I'm too tall—"

"Whoa, calm down." She sensed she'd surprised him, but Ben wouldn't let her go. He held her close when she would have struggled away, and she remembered how very strong he was. In the past, it had been exciting, but now she was too weary, too drained and disgruntled for it to register.

"Let me go. I want to go home." She knew she sounded petulant, but she was beyond caring.

"No. You're upset. Tell me what's wrong."

"I can't. It's not—" To her dismay, her breath began to hitch and her voice wobbled. A tear rolled down her cheek as she gazed at him mutely, appealing to him without words to let her go.

His expression altered and he groaned. "Don't cry." He lowered his head and kissed her eyes closed. "I can't stand it when you cry."

She knew that. He never had been able to deal with her tears. It was one of the things that had driven a wedge between them after her tubal ligation. But she couldn't stop the flow of tears. She felt weak and lethargic, totally drained of willpower.

When his mouth slid down her cheek to capture

hers, she didn't resist. He kissed her lightly, softly, over and over again, until her tears were forgotten. Small flames of heat began to curl in her abdomen; she leaned into him and kissed him back. At the first sign of her participation, he deepened the kiss, using his tongue to skillfully probe and tease until her breath was coming as fast as his and she was twisting in his arms, following his mouth each time it shifted over hers. When he lightly ran his hands from her back around to the sides of her waist, then slid them up to palm her breasts, she brought her own hands up to cover his, pressing him against her sensitive flesh in clear invitation.

"I want you." The words were a rough growl against her lips. "No more waiting."

She wanted him, too. As he swept her into his arms and carried her down the hallway to the door of his bedroom, she couldn't remember a single good reason why she'd thought they needed to wait. Carrying her into the room, he slowly released the arm beneath her knees and let her slide down his body. As he gathered her against him, he took her mouth again in a deep, drugging kiss.

Ben was shaking, so great was his need for her. His fingers fumbled with the small buttons down the back of the practical dress she'd worn to work today. Impatient, he grasped the fabric in both hands and she felt the satisfying slack of the material as the buttons popped off and went flying. She gasped and he laughed deep in his throat as he took her down to the bed beneath him.

He wrestled her out of the dress and removed her undergarments with swift surety, petting and caressing her with each movement, stroking her legs, her belly, her breasts until she was mindless. She reached for him with frantic hands that sought the fulfillment only he could provide.

He levered himself away from her and stripped off his own clothes before rejoining her. Propping herself on one elbow, she drank in the sight of his naked body. She hadn't gotten to look her fill the first time they'd made love and she stared openly, fascinated anew by the muscles that rippled down his arms, his flat stomach and strong legs, the proof of his desire that sprang so boldly from the thatch of black curls at his thighs. She knew he exercised faithfully at a health club nearby and his body proved it; she couldn't wait to touch him, to run her hands over all that hardness and heat.

But when she held up her arms to welcome him, he grasped her wrists and held them above her head, surveying the tender curves he'd bared with hot intent in his gaze.

Ben could read the invitation in her eyes, but as he watched, her gaze shifted away from his skittishly. When he released her wrists to come down beside her, she made a hasty motion to shield herself, covering her breasts with crossed arms. He suddenly had a vivid mental image of her embarrassment the first time he'd made love to her.

"Why are you hiding this beautiful body?" Gently,

but inexorably, he circled her wrists with his fingers and pried her arms away from her body.

Her face was flushed and she wouldn't meet his eyes. "I'm different now," she said in a stifled tone.

"Different?" Deliberately he pretended not to understand.

"Don't be obtuse," she said with a hint of asperity, the first sign of spirit he'd seen tonight. "Carrie had big breasts—breasts you loved. I don't even need to wear a bra now! And my hair—this fine, flyaway stuff—I know how much you loved my long hair...."

"And you think those things are going to be a problem for me? That I won't love this body?"

Her voice caught and her eyes filled again. "I—I don't know what to think. Sometimes I want you to want me, sometimes it makes me...mad."

Tenderly he traced the silky skin along her cheekbones with one finger. "It's *you* I fell in love with, not your other body, although that certainly got me interested in the beginning. Yeah, this body's different—"

He paused as the familiar guilt intruded. But they had to put it behind them. Deliberately he ran a caressing hand down one long sleek thigh and pulled it up to hook it intimately around his back. The contact made him grit his teeth as he tried to block out the overwhelming desire to plunge into the soft, moist heat he could feel. Desperately he hung on to the thoughts he'd been voicing.

"This body's equally exciting in other ways." *And in a minute he was going to prove it.* He kissed a path from the smooth line of her jaw down her neck and onto the slope of one sweet mound, fastening his lips over the pink tip and suckling gently.

Marina cried out, arching against him, involuntarily stroking his aroused flesh against her belly with the motion. He gritted his teeth again, loving the sweet torture, afraid he wasn't going to be able to prolong it like he wanted.

"These legs..." He was panting as he caressed the firm thigh surrounding him. "These wonderful, beautiful, mile-long legs."

Marina relaxed under his warm hands and the honest pleasure in his voice. He didn't sound like a man who was disappointed with her body. When he slipped a hand between their bodies and ran it firmly, purposefully, over the swell of her belly to the curly nest at the junction of her thighs, she shuddered. He pressed on, curving his fingers down and under until he'd found her, probing and pressing. She knew she was ready, felt the excitement poised within her awaiting release, and she wriggled her hips against him. "Take me."

He needed no second invitation. Rearing back, he let the tip of his engorged flesh lie snug against the tight opening of her body. She wriggled again, drawing him into the warm channel, and he pushed forcefully forward in one eager stroke, embedding himself deeply within her.

The full sensation, the slick glide of his flesh within her as he established his rhythm, made her want to scream. She surged upward repeatedly, increasing speed, throwing her head back and forth on the pillow as the assault on her senses overtook her. When she reached her peak, he captured the sounds she made with his own mouth, holding her close and shuddering as her body tightened and released, tightened and released around him. She had barely begun to relax when he pushed her limp thighs farther apart and succumbed to his own driving pace, lasting only moments until he was shouting out his own completion as his body spent itself within her.

It was perfect. *He* was perfect. Why had she thought they should forego their physical loving? Suddenly all her carefully thought-out reasons seemed illogical and idiotic. This was why she had been born. And reborn.

"Am I too heavy?" His voice echoed satiation and satisfaction.

He was heavy, but she didn't want him to move. "No, I'm fine." Remembering how much he enjoyed having his back scratched, she ran her nails leisurely up and down his spine and out across each shoulder blade.

"Mmm." He groaned appreciatively as she repeated the movements again and again.

She smiled and reached down with one hand to draw the sheets up over their rapidly cooling bodies. As she did so, the pale oak shade of the bed in which they lay caught her eye.

"Why did you get rid of our bed?" She blurted out the question without intending to sound accusatory, but Ben stiffened immediately. Darn it. Why had she said that? She'd loved the brass bed in which Jennie was conceived, but she loved Ben more. It wasn't as if it was important.

Sliding from her, he rolled onto his back and stared at the ceiling. For a long time, he didn't speak and she thought he was going to ignore the question.

Finally he sighed and she was struck by the almost hopeless quality of the sound. "I couldn't stand it without Carrie."

She was moved by the simple statement. "I'm sorry I asked. It's not a big deal."

But he went on as if he hadn't heard her, his voice harsh with pain remembered. "Every time I came into this room, I'd see her...you. Sitting propped up among the pillows nursing Jennie. Cuddled into a ball in the middle after I'd come back in from running in the morning. Sitting on the edge with nothing but your unbound hair covering you. I just couldn't take it. I slept on the sofa for a month before I decided to sell it and get this. I knew how much you'd loved it. I was going to keep it for Jennie, but the memories were too painful." He exhaled a ragged sigh and threw an arm over his eyes. "We can get a new one if you want."

"Ben..." Hesitantly she rolled onto her left side and laid her palm in the center of his chest. Could they ever get past all these old wounds? Each of them had been indelibly altered by dissimilar, but equally stressful experiences—were they foolish to hope to repair what had been irrevocably shattered? "This bed is beautiful. But we can sleep on the floor for all I care, as long as I'm with you.''

He didn't answer her immediately. Finally he laid his hand over hers, squeezing her fingers so tightly they hurt. ''I love you. That's all that's important.'' He rolled toward her and took her into his arms, cradling her against his big body. ''We can decide later about the bed. It might be nice to buy a new one together, sort of a celebration of our new life. And then again...'' He pulled her over on top of him, and she could feel the quickening of his body pushing at her belly. ''I could grow to like this bed.''

She was awakened just after dawn by the sound of Major whining. She slipped quickly out of Ben's bed, shivering in the morning chill. Grabbing his robe and cinching the belt as she went, she let the dog out through the utility room door and returned to the bedroom.

With a guilty pang, she remembered her own pets. Lucky surely needed to go out by now. Quietly she discarded the robe and snatched up her underclothes. As she stepped into the tiny peach panties she'd worn the day before, two big hands grasped her around the waist and toppled her back onto the bed. She squeaked in surprise, remembering just before she let out a scream that Jennie slept in a room down the hall.

''Where do you think you're going?'' a gravelly morning voice growled in her ear.

''Lucky will need to go out.'' She was breathless and her pulse pounded as the hands slid up her torso to rub gentle circles over her breasts and a hard male body pressed against her back. "Oh, that feels so good...." She grasped the hands. "But I really have to go."

"Will you come right back?" Ben's hands stilled and he nipped at her neck before he released her. "Bring the damned animals with you. They're going to be a part of this family soon. And I don't want to sleep without you another night."

Turning to him, she was confronted by the sight of his powerfully aroused body blatantly displayed on the bed before her. She swallowed, wanting nothing more than to crawl back in with him and let him touch her in all the intimate places that were throbbing, longing for his stroking assuagement. "All right."

She took a quick shower while Lucky ran around the backyard. Then, dressed in clean clothes and feeling infinitely less grungy, she gathered up Cloud, her white cat, and put Lucky on a leash before heading back over to Ben's.

When she opened the door with the key he'd given her, the first thing she heard was the television.

"M'rina!" Jennie came dashing out to the foyer, skidding to an openmouthed stop as she registered the animals. "Daddy!" She turned and raced back the way she had come, squealing at the top of her lungs. "Daddy! M'rina bringed her dog-gie and her kittie to me's house!"

Ben appeared in the hallway, grinning ruefully. "Our morning plans have been superceded by an early-rising midget." He scooped up his daughter in one arm and cautioned, "Shh. You'll scare Marina's pets if you shout."

"Why M'rina bring her pets to me's house?"

It was the perfect opening. Ben's gaze met Marina's and she nodded. *Tell her.* Jennie needed time to get used to the idea of Marina moving in, but not so much time that it became an interminable wait for the small child.

Ben knelt and set Jennie on the floor, then stroked Cloud as she wandered over to sniff him. "Do you like Marina's pets, Jen?"

"Uh-huh." Jennie was more interested in following the cat than in what her father was saying.

Ben took a deep breath and Marina could feel the tension he was trying to hide. "Marina and her dog and cat are going to move in with us."

"M'rina live with me?"

"That's right."

Jennie was silent for a minute. Then she looked at Marina. "You s'eep wif me?"

Marina felt her face growing red. "No, honey," she said gently. "I'll sleep in Daddy's bed."

"Daddy's bed is bigger." To Jennie, this was the logical explanation.

Ben knelt beside his daughter. "Jennie, Marina would like to be your mommy. Would you like that?"

Silence again. Then, "Me have two mommies. M'rina my mommy here. My other mommy goed away wif God."

"That's right." Marina knelt, too, and held out her arms, feeling the sting of tears. "I love you, Peanut."

Jennie willingly ran over for a kiss and cuddle, then she leaned back in Marina's arms. "Mommy needs a baby. We get a baby at me's house?"

Behind her, Ben gave a strangled laugh. "We'll talk about babies another day, Jen. Let's go let Major and Lucky out in the backyard so they can play."

Baby. As Ben and Jennie vanished down the hallway with the dog, Marina sat slowly back on her heels. *Oh, my God. Birth control.*

Ben came back into the hallway. "Jennie has to finish her breakfast. Then I thought we could get out the Christmas decorations—since we'll have to postpone what I'd rather be doing." He eyed her figure in a suggestive way.

She didn't even smile as she rose. "Ben, we need to use birth control. I'm not protected. I—I could already be pregnant."

For an instant, Ben looked as shocked as she felt. "My God, I could kick myself." Then his brow cleared and he smiled. She could see the dawning realization in his eyes as he understood that her new body wasn't sterile. "Why should it matter? We're getting married."

"It matters to me," she flared. "The rest of the world believes we only met two months ago, remember? We need time to adjust to being together again before we do anything hasty."

"We've already been hasty, honey. And it was good, remember?" He gave her a roguish grin as he pulled her against him.

She softened a little, her voice dropping. "It *was* good, wasn't it? I love you, Ben."

"And I love you." He kissed her with lingering intent, then drew away reluctantly. "I'll handle the birth control for now. But I wouldn't mind a little 'Oops.' Another baby would be great. And Jennie would be the perfect age for a new sibling."

"Ben!" She was exasperated and she let it show as she crossed her arms, clutching her elbows tightly. "Jennie needs time to get used to me. I'm thrilled at the thought of being able to give you more children, but this is not the ideal time."

He threw up his hands in a gesture of surrender. "I get the message. I'm willing to wait a few months and discuss this when we're more relaxed."

She allowed him to turn her toward the kitchen as he spoke, to change the subject to Jennie's Christmas and pretend that nothing was wrong. But beneath the surface, she worried over the new seed of discord. It wouldn't be weeded out of their marriage as easily as the conversation. The very fact that Ben assumed she'd be ready to have another baby mere months from now bothered her. What about her store?

His mother joined them for dinner on Sunday. Over dessert, while Jennie was occupied with her ice cream, Ben cleared his throat. "Mother, Marina and I have an announcement to make."

When Helen laid down her spoon and looked across the table at him, he placed his hand over Marina's, where she sat at his left side. "Marina and I have decided to get married in the new year. We know everything's happened quickly between us, but we're sure of our feelings." He paused, unable to read his mother's expression. "I hope we'll have your blessing."

Very slowly, Helen picked up her napkin and touched it to her lips before she spoke. Marina's fingers were tense under his; he squeezed them gently in reassurance.

Then his mother said, "If anyone had told me that I'd be pleased to have my widowed son declaring his intentions to remarry six months later, I'd have said they were crazy." She smiled and the corners of her lips trembled. "But I am pleased. No, make that delighted. You two deserve to be happy and I can see that you're good for each other. Of course you have my blessing. I'd better be invited to the wedding!" She came out of her chair and walked around the table to kiss him. Then she turned to Marina, and Ben could see the sheen of tears in both women's eyes. "Welcome to the family, dear. I hope you'll think of me as a mother."

Marina stood in a rush and hugged Helen convulsively. "Thank you. Your approval means so much."

"All right, no mushy stuff." What would he do if they both cried at once?

As one, they turned to him and laughed. "You're so predictable," Helen said with a sniff.

"But cute." Marina patted him on the head as if he were five years old and he glared at her, promising retribution when they were alone. She only smiled as she took a load of dishes out to the kitchen.

Returning to her seat, Helen smiled fondly at the top of Jennie's bent head. The child was industriously shoveling ice cream into her mouth and Ben noticed with amusement that she was wearing quite a bit of it, too.

"This will be good for her," Helen said softly. "And truthfully, it will be a relief to me to have some time for myself again. I love her dearly, but she's exhausting sometimes."

"I hope you won't abandon us completely," Ben teased, but she gave him a serious look.

"You know you can always rely on me to help out with Jennie whenever you need me."

"You're welcome to visit anytime, but we should only need the occasional sitter after Marina's home again," he replied.

Helen threw him a puzzled look. "Again? I thought she'd had her store for quite a while."

The slip shook him. He'd have to watch what he said around his mother. "She has. I only meant after I have a wife at home again."

"So Marina is going to give up the store?"

She had touched on a subject that was most definitely a sore spot between him and Marina, and he shifted uncomfortably under his mother's scrutiny. "We haven't discussed the details yet—"

"Ben." Her voice was as stern as it had been when she'd caught him in some of his worst childhood escapades. "Marina isn't Carrie. I hope you won't try to force her into a mold she isn't made to fit."

But that was where she was wrong. *Marina was Carrie.* "Mother, I—"

"I know why it's so important to you to have your wife at home. I'm sorry if your childhood wasn't everything you would have wished because I was gone so much." She straightened her shoulders and despite his irritation he was oddly touched by the small movement. "But it made you the man you are today, a man of whom I'm very proud."

His pique vanished as fast as it had arisen. She hadn't meant to anger him. "Thanks, Mom."

She smiled smugly. "I think Marina will be good for you. I loved Carrie very much, but sometimes I worried that she never stood up to you. Carrie lived so completely for you and Jennie that if anything had happened to either of you, I don't know what she'd have done." Helen's voice quavered, then grew stronger. "I'm thankful that, if this horrible accident had to happen, it didn't take you. Yes, because you're my only child, but also because I'm not sure Carrie could have survived without you."

His mother's words were almost shocking. He hadn't seen Carrie that way. Guilt descended. If his mother had perceived his wife in that light, it was only because Carrie had loved him so very much— and he hadn't valued that love. He'd hurt her deeply. Stark memories of the last days of Carrie's life came to him. How easy it was now to see that she hadn't been happy.

He'd been the one who'd made her miserable. She'd blamed herself for not being able to give him more children. And, battling his own disappointment, he hadn't made the effort to reassure her as he should have.

An ugly thought reared its head. He'd carefully managed to beat it back in the past, but now, today, it confronted him squarely. They'd been arguing on the way to the park that day...he couldn't even remember why anymore. It had been a meaningless quarrel, but lurking beneath it had been...what?

Had he been harboring a subconscious desire to punish her for denying him a big family? It was hard to face, hard to accept. Even harder was the memory of seeing Carrie lying beneath the wheel of that truck, hearing Jennie's hysterical screams as he'd handed her to a compassionate passerby and raced to his wife. If he'd been paying attention to the traffic instead of focusing on his own petty grievances, could he have prevented what happened? Might Carrie be alive today—in her own body?

Christmas was only a week away. Kids' Place had been busy every minute of every day they'd been open. Gratified by the rapidly emptying stockroom she was surveying, Marina made notes about popular items to reorder.

She set down her clipboard as a wave of exhaustion swamped her. Wow. She'd been working hard lately. Trying to keep up with her housework, her own

Christmas preparations and making sure Jennie fully experienced the season weren't helping.

Feeling as if she needed some fresh air, she slowly pushed open the stockroom door and entered the store. She groped for the stool behind the counter and lowered herself onto it. If only she could put her head down and close her eyes for a few minutes...

"Marina! Are you all right?" Jillian's voice penetrated her stupor, and an arm circled her back. "Here, sit up and let me look at you."

Hazily Marina realized she had dropped her head to the counter. Had she been dozing? "I'm okay," she mumbled.

"Only if your name is Sleeping Beauty," Jill responded with asperity. "Do you feel ill?"

"No." She managed to shake off the worst of the sleepiness. "I'm just so tired. Guess I've been overdoing it a little."

"I guess." Jill didn't sound convinced. "Why don't you go home and sleep for the rest of the day? If you don't get your energy back, maybe you should go to the doctor. You could have mono or something."

Or something. If she had what she suspected, the only thing that would cure her was time. About eight months of it, to be specific.

She went home as Jillian suggested. Crawling into the oak bed was heavenly. Her body gave a nearly audible sigh of relief. She hadn't slept at the other house in days. In fact they'd turned off the utilities and were gradually moving the things she wanted to keep.

Before she dropped off to sleep, she opened the drawer of the bedside table and pulled out the small calendar she kept there. It had been one of the first things she'd brought over, and she knew what it said by heart, but she counted anyway. She was just over six weeks late. Forty-four days, to be exact. Her last normal cycle had been in early November.

If she had conceived, it had been in late November, before Ben had started using birth control...about four weeks ago. Maybe she should get one of those little kits and find out for sure. End this agony of waiting. Ben deserved to know.

She smiled sheepishly, anticipating his excitement. Funny how her feelings had changed in the past few weeks. A baby right now wasn't the best idea, she knew, but it no longer mattered. She loved Ben and having another baby, regardless of how other people might perceive it, would cement their new relationship in a way that nothing else could. She placed a hand protectively over her abdomen as her eyes closed. A baby...

Something was tickling her ear. She lifted a hand and wafted it in the air above her ear...

...and connected with warm, rough flesh. She opened her eyes. Her hand rested along Ben's cheek. His big body was gingerly perched on about two inches of the mattress. Scooting over, she gave him some room.

"You feeling okay?" His face registered concern.

"I called the store to talk to you and Jillian said you'd gone home to get some rest."

"I'm okay." She didn't want to raise his hopes if this was a false alarm. "Just tired. But I feel better now. What time is it?"

When he named a time in the middle of the afternoon, her eyes widened. "Holy cow! I came home just before ten." Then she remembered he'd said he'd called her. "Why did you call me?"

"I thought that we could take some time today to wrap Jennie's Christmas presents while she's with Mom. Then we don't have to stay up so late on Christmas Eve."

Before Jennie was born, they'd opened their gifts on Christmas Eve and slept in the next morning. But since Jennie came along, that routine had altered. "Good idea. I've got my energy back now."

"Oh, yeah?" His tone was seductive as he bent to fit his lips to hers.

"Yeah." She slid her arms around his neck and tugged until he lay full-length on the bed, half over her, covers between them. Even so, she could feel the strength and heat of his body and her own responded by softening and changing, preparing for his sweet invasion. "Wanna unwrap me first?"

Nine

The next evening, Marina did the dishes while Ben gave Jennie her bath. After the little girl had been tucked into bed, Ben placed an arm around Marina's shoulders as they walked down the hallway toward the family room.

"Christmas will be here in three days. Maybe we should talk about a date for our wedding."

She rested her head against his shoulder for an instant, loving the solid strength of him. "The sooner the better."

"New Year's Eve."

She stopped and turned to face him. "What?"

"New Year's Eve. For our wedding."

She smiled and shook her head. "I know it's going to be a small ceremony with just your mother, my sister and Jennie, but don't you think you're rushing it a bit? That's only nine days away.''

"So? What needs to be done?"

She thought of all the things that had to happen to pull off a wedding, then realized that most of them would be superfluous for the intimate ceremony they'd discussed. ''A few flowers, a meal somewhere, a photographer. All right, I guess that's not so much. But will the pastor marry us on New Year's Eve? And what about a license?''

"I've already checked." He sounded smug. "We can be married forty-eight hours from the time I apply for a license, with no blood work necessary."

Excitement rose, and she stepped forward to give him an impulsive hug. ''I'd be delighted to marry you on New Year's Eve.''

"I was hoping you'd say yes. I'll take care of the paperwork tomorrow and call the pastor."

"Wonderful. I can wear my old rings if they still fit."

Ben grinned and shook his head. ''I'll buy you new ones. People would talk if you wore Carrie's rings.''

"People are going to talk anyway," she predicted, laying her head against his shoulder again and looping her arms around his neck. ''They're going to criticize both of us for marrying with indecent haste.''

"I don't give a flying damn." Ben shifted her so that their bodies fit snugly, tilting her face up to give her a kiss that was fierce with need. ''I'm not putting this off one more day than we have to. We've already lost half a year together.''

"But we got a second chance," she reminded him, running her palms up under his shirt to caress the strong muscles of his back.

"Thank God," Ben muttered, sounding as if he meant it. Then he leaned away from her slightly, smiling down at her. "Now that we have a wedding date, you can make plans to resign. If Jillian wants to buy your half of the shop, we'll come to some agreement that won't strap her. You're going to have your hands full with your family again."

Marina frowned, stiffening in his arms. She didn't want to have this conversation here, now, without planning what she would say, but she had no choice. "Ben, I'm thinking of continuing to work at the shop part-time. I have responsibilities there. Jillian needs me."

Ben's body had stiffened, as well. He dropped his arms from around her and his voice was accusatory when he said, "Jennie and I need you, too. And you have plenty of responsibilities here to keep you busy."

"I've been thinking of hiring someone to come in and clean," she said in a low voice. "Then I could manage the house and still keep an active interest in the store."

He threw her an incredulous look. "That's ridiculous. And unnecessary, when you don't need to work. I can take care of us. It's not as if we need the money." He spread his hands in a pleading gesture. "I don't understand why you suddenly feel compelled to play shopkeeper. You were happy enough before."

"Was I?" She swallowed, and it felt as if a ball of sandpaper were lodged in her throat. "Ben, please try to understand. It isn't you. I might never have worked if I'd stayed Carrie Bradford. But I didn't. And the woman I've become is someone I like. Kids' Place challenges me. And I feel good about the fact that I've risen to that challenge."

Ben didn't respond, and her heart sank a little as he stared at her with hot, resentful eyes.

"I love you," she said desperately. "The way I feel about you has nothing to with my desire to work at the shop. I hope your feelings for me aren't predicated on having a meek little wife who's home all day every day."

Her words stung. They reminded him of what his mother had said only the night before. Guilt made him defensive. "Of course they aren't. I haven't had much time to get used to the idea of having a career woman for a wife."

"I know you can provide for your family." She stepped toward him and placed her hands on his shoulders. "The shop is something I need in here." Her hand smote her breast in a passionate gesture. "Not to pay the bills, not to get away from the children or to retain independence from you, but simply because I've found that I love the experience. Do you know what I mean?"

It took everything he had not to turn away from her. The seed of hope that had blossomed in his heart since her return withered and died as he realized that nothing he could say would change her mind now.

Even if they had another baby, she wouldn't be willing to stay home. And he wasn't willing to bring another child into the world under those circumstances.

Aloud, he said, "No. I don't understand. I thought being my wife and the mother of my children was a job in itself, that you were fulfilled in those roles." Slowly his hands came up to clasp her arms, and his thumbs caressed the fragile flesh of her inner wrists as he wrestled with himself, torn between love and disappointment. He sighed. "I'll be honest—having a working wife doesn't thrill me. I foresee a lot of hassles with child care, house care, meals, vacation schedules...." His voice trailed away. "And I can't imagine how we'd work another baby into the equation."

She almost told him of her suspicions then. Almost. But the note of despondency she heard in his tone aroused her instincts to comfort, to provide solace in a world that had changed around him through no fault of his own.

She reached for his hand, relieved when he didn't pull away. Couldn't he see that they could overcome anything? That their worst nightmares had been lived and conquered? Dear God, had he any inkling of how much she loved him?

Slowly her thumb glided back and forth in a soothing caress across his hair-roughened skin. Her gaze was steady on his as she carried his hand to her mouth. "We'll work it out. I promise." Greatly daring, she nibbled at the base of his thumb, then ran her tongue slowly up to the tip of his index finger until she could take it into her mouth and gently suckle.

The pain eased from his eyes like a shadow being chased by the sun; his eyelids drooped and grew heavy lidded as he watched her work her way across his hand, licking and sucking at each of his fingers in turn. She could hear his breath rush in and out of his lungs and the sounds of his arousal sent waves of excitement straight to her abdomen, where they lodged in a tight ball. Every breath she took quivered with the heady taste of feminine power. She wasn't normally aggressive; Ben had always taken the lead in their loving.

"Let's go to bed," she murmured against his palm.

Linking her fingers through his, she led him down the hallway into the shadowed room with the oak bed she'd refused to allow him to remove. When they reached the middle of the bedroom she stopped, shaking her head and stepping skittishly back when he lifted his hand to caress her. "Wait. Let me."

He stood like a statue, with only the leaping flame in his eyes to warn her of the great restraint her request imposed on him. Slowly she stepped a pace away, then another, leaving her shoes behind. An ingrained shyness, coupled with a renewed burst of insecurity about her new body, nearly halted her, but she forced herself to ignore it, focusing on the heat in his gaze for reassurance. She found it. Silver-blue and blazing, his eyes narrowed as his nostrils flared in rhythm with his heavy breathing.

Lifting a hand, she released each of the tiny pearl

buttons that ran down the front of her businesslike cotton blouse. His gaze was riveted to the shadowed opening appearing as the fabric fell apart. He licked his lips and his chest rose and fell. Marina smiled. She shrugged her shoulders and the blouse fell away, revealing the lacy ivory camisole and matching bra she'd worn beneath it.

Her lined skirt and panty hose came next, leaving her clad in tiny French-cut panties that matched the rest of her lingerie. Silently she thanked the first Marina for her exotic taste in underwear. As she walked across the few feet of space toward Ben, his Adam's apple bobbed and his fists clenched. Hoarsely he accused, "Tease."

She laughed, the husky siren call of a woman suddenly sure of her charm. "Shall I stop?"

"Come here." It was a guttural demand.

One step took her close. Two brought her breasts against his chest, her hips against his strong thighs. Boldly she insinuated the flat of her palm between them, finding the zipper of his wool pants stretched to bursting, feeling the leaping proof of his intentions pushing into her hand. Smiling as she looked into his eyes, she rubbed in a small up-and-down, up-and-down movement and he groaned. Startled by the harsh, agonized sound, she pulled her hand away.

"Don't stop. Don't stop." Almost frantically he grasped her hand and positioned it against himself, using his palm over hers to communicate the rhythm of his need.

She was more aroused by his excitement than she

could have believed. Between her legs, an insistent throbbing distracted her. Her nipples were taut and turgid, aching for stimulation, and she stripped away his shirt, then rubbed herself back and forth over his chest, loving the feel of his crisp hair against her. When he shifted position and pushed one of his legs between hers, she didn't protest. Eagerly she accepted the press of his thigh against her throbbing mound, eagerly she initiated a rocking motion that gave her a measure of relief from the raging desire ripping through her.

His breath came in shallow pants now and his head was thrown back, his handsome features contorted as he gave himself to her small, stroking palm.

She loved the feel of him through his pants, rock-hard and solid, but it wasn't enough.

Bringing her other hand up, she tore at the fastenings of his trousers. The button at his waistband popped. His zipper hissed down the track, releasing his swollen flesh from confinement, and he groaned again.

When she delved into his briefs and closed her hand around his hot, silky shaft, his breath whistled out in a curse, and when she gently pulled him free, his teeth snapped together and he sucked air back in abruptly.

"Oh, yes." It was a moaning, keening plea. His big hands gripped her shoulders, then feverishly traveled up and down her back in mindless patterns. When his fingers caught in the lace of her camisole, he tugged upward until the camisole was rucked up under her arms and he could reach the single clasp of her bra in the middle of her back.

She knew a moment of cutting pressure as the stretchy elastic resisted his efforts. Then she was blessedly free and he was tearing her remaining clothes over her head in a mad rush, kneeling to pull down the tiny panties until she stood before him completely, gloriously nude.

He didn't rise immediately from his kneeling position before her. Again, some imp of femininity took over and she widened her stance before him, thrusting her pelvis forward in an invitation he was quick to catch. He reached for her, clasping big hands around her buttocks, holding her in place with an inflexible grip as he pressed his mouth against the nest of downy curls at the V of her legs.

She gasped as a hot breath seared her and her hands came up to clench in his hair. An instant later, she felt the teasing flick of his tongue as he sought out the tight nub of need buried within her soft folds. She cried out as he probed and licked, locking her knees when they felt as if they might give away. Then he pushed his mouth more tightly against her and she was shocked to feel teeth close over her most sensitive flesh.

She tried to pull back, instinctively protective, but he laughed deep in his throat, and held her in place, giving his tongue free rein to plunder and pummel the sweet treasure he'd captured. She moaned and swayed. Her consciousness receded, and there was only him, only the touch of his tongue and his teeth and his hands on her. In her belly, a knot of force was growing, gathering momentum, fed by the wild demands he made on her body.

It would be so easy to let go, to give him the ultimate surrender he sought, but she resisted, unwilling to give herself over to his domination, needing to be an equal partner in this exchange. Her fingers plunged deep into his hair and tightened, until he gave a hoarse groan and released her, letting his head fall back.

Looking down at his body, she could see stiff, proud flesh rising from his loins where he knelt before her. The sight fueled the fires inside her and she took him by the shoulders, pressing him backward until he acquiesced and stretched out full-length before her.

She knelt astride him, surveying with urgent pleasure the signs of his desire. Lowering herself, she pinioned him beneath her and rubbed her body back and forth over rigid, satiny manflesh. He shuddered, his back arching, and his arousal sprang free to boldly thrust at her. He raised his hands and placed them at her hips and his thumbs came to rest again on the slippery, swollen knot of nerves he'd been loving a moment before.

Her body shouted its demands at her, begging for what she knew he could provide, and she waited no longer. Raising herself on her knees, she arched her hips forward, snaring him in one silken slide that thrust him deep inside her when she dropped her weight over him. If she'd been less involved, she'd have been embarrassed at the ease with which her body welcomed him.

"Ahhh..." His eyes were squeezed tightly shut; she could feel him throbbing inside her.

Again she lifted and dropped herself, feeling the shove and release of wonderful male pressure impaling her with each movement. Her breathing was ragged now too, and she moaned as she lifted herself again and yet again, picking up the pace with each repetition until they were a single frantic unit, straining and moving together.

Completion was only seconds away. She could feel herself gathering speed, rushing to meet temporary oblivion. When his body suddenly roared into overdrive beneath her, the slamming thrusts of his climax sent her spinning over the edge to tighten repeatedly around him, milking him with uncontrollable, shuddering contractions until they were both shaking and weak.

Slowly, unable to summon any energy, she let herself fall forward to rest on his chest, realizing only then that they lay in the middle of the carpeted room. For long, long moments, they simply lay, gathering strength, feeling the occasional, breathtaking pulse of the other's body as they quivered with aftershocks.

Finally she raised herself on her arms and propped them on his chest so she could see his eyes. "Wow."

Amusement flared in the blue depths. "Yeah. That just about covers it. Where did you learn to be such a tigress?"

She shrugged. "It felt right."

"It certainly did."

She started to reply, then was halted by an involuntary shiver. "Brr. It's cold down here on the floor."

"Let's go to bed." With gentle hands, Ben lifted her off him and rose to his feet, extending a hand to pull her up. As he did so, he suddenly cursed vividly.

She was startled by the change in his relaxed features. He looked harsh, forbidding, as angry as he had earlier. "What's the matter?"

"We forgot something." Crudely he gestured at his uncovered flesh, slackening now with temporary satiation.

"Birth control." She smiled, hoping to reassure him. "It doesn't matter."

"It does to me. Until we work out our plans, *it does to me.*" He released her hand and turned toward the bathroom. "Get in bed."

She stood beside the oak bed as he vanished into the bathroom, then slowly folded back the covers and climbed in. A cold, stony weight settled in her stomach. He'd sounded so final. *What would he say about the baby?*

She stared at the ceiling with sightless eyes, feeling the cocoon of blankets warming around her. A minute later, the bathroom door opened and the light was snapped off. Ben strode across the room and a blast of cooler air poured over her as he slid in on his side.

Tentatively she reached out a hand and laid it on his chest. His skin was chilly, but as he turned toward her and enfolded her in his arms, her relief was too great to care.

"I love you," she whispered against his chest.

"I love you, too." He dropped a whisper-light kiss on the top of her head.

As his breathing slowed and his body relaxed, she decided she'd definitely get one of those kits tomorrow. Ben loved her. He might be feeling threatened and upset about her job, but they'd work out the problems. He'd be thrilled about a baby.

She was only scheduled to work until one o'clock the day before Christmas Eve, but the hours seemed to crawl by. Every time Marina checked her watch, she swore she'd wait longer before she checked it again.

More than once, she caught Jillian watching her furtively. Finally, when her sister gave her a sheepish grin, Marina demanded, "What? Have I grown a horn in the middle of my forehead?"

"Just wondered how you were feeling. No need to get touchy." Jill busily applied a feather duster to a display of children's train sets.

Marina started. Then she realized Jill was thinking of her sleepiness yesterday. "I feel fine." She knew she was grinning like a fool, but she couldn't help it. She was almost positive she was pregnant. The glow faded a bit as she thought of Ben's face last night after they'd made love, but she thrust the image determinedly out of her head. He'd be so excited. Maybe it would be a son this time, a little guy he could teach to play baseball or golf.

The minute the hands of the clock ticked into place,

she grabbed her coat and purse. "See you tomorrow."

"Don't be late," Jill called after her. "We're always busy on Christmas Eve."

"So you've said. Don't worry, I'll be here."

She made one stop at a pharmacy on the way home. It took longer than she'd expected. Who'd have ever thought there'd be so many brands of pregnancy-test kits? She finally selected one that she could use immediately without waiting for morning and hurried back to her car.

At home, all three of the animals greeted her enthusiastically. Dropping her coat on the long bench in the foyer, she petted each of them briefly, amazed as always at how easily Major had accepted the two intruders in his home. Then, giving Cloud a final stroke, she went on to the bedroom with her precious package.

A short while later, she had her answer.

A baby! She'd thought she was sure, but seeing the proof of it now was overwhelming. Tears of joy stung her eyes. She jumped off the side of the bed where she'd been sitting and whirled around the room, then impulsively snatched up the phone.

Ben's secretary put her through right away.

"Ben Bradford."

His deep voice made her smile and warmed her heart. "Hello, Ben Bradford."

"Hi." His tone was intimate. "I was just thinking about you."

"Oh? Anything you can share over the phone?"

He laughed shortly. "Definitely not." Then a pause. "Where are you?"

She kept her voice low, seductive. "Home."

"Jennie's still with Mom?"

"Uh-huh. I had a few things to do before I picked her up."

"Anything that requires my assistance?" He was smiling; she could hear it in his voice.

"Most certainly. Can you get away?"

There was a sound of a desk drawer closing. "It's a slow afternoon. I was thinking of packing it in soon anyway. I'll be home in twenty minutes."

"Don't get arrested for speeding."

It was a miracle he hadn't, she thought when he walked in the door less than half an hour later. She'd been sitting in the family room, rehearsing what she would say, and she leapt to her feet as he entered the house.

"Hi!"

He looked at her quizzically, slinging his coat over a chair. "Don't sound so surprised. I distinctly remember you calling me and luring me home."

She giggled nervously, not sure how to begin now that the important moment was at hand. Should she ask him to sit down? Maybe. She seated herself on the couch.

He was already advancing across the rug with a blatantly sexual gleam in his eye. "It's not often we have the house to ourselves. Shall we have a party for two in front of the fire?"

It sounded tempting, it really did. But she wanted

to tell him first so they could celebrate together. "Ben, will you sit down?" She patted the cushion beside her invitingly.

He stopped in front of her. "Want me to build a fire first?"

"No." Jumping up, she threw her arms around his neck, feeling his instant reaction as he hugged her close. She whispered in his ear, "I have some very, very good news for you."

He was still. "What?"

"Can't you guess?"

He pulled back slightly and gauged her expression. "No guesses. But it's sure made you happy."

She waited.

He paused.

She leaned forward and touched her lips to his. "You're going to be a daddy again."

"What?"

She laughed. "I said, you're—" But the words died in her throat as he reached up and ripped her arms from around his neck.

Roughly he pushed her away and stepped back a pace. "You're pregnant?"

"Yes." Fear choked her, but she forced out the words. "I've only missed once, but I took one of those home tests and I'm nearly certain. It must have happened that very first time." *Please tell me you want this baby. Please, God, let him tell me he wants this child.*

Ben clenched his hands and unclenched them, spinning to look out the French doors at the lawn. "Jeez."

She would not cry. She would not. Anger took over and she welcomed it, afraid the fear and misery would conquer her if she let them. "That's all you can say? 'Jeez?'"

He swiveled again and she fell back a pace at the rage in his eyes. "What do you expect me to say, Marina? It's hard to be thrilled about another baby when you don't even have time for the one we have. Babies need a lot of care, remember? Who's going to take care of this kid while you're working in your precious store?" The bitter words cut the air between them like a newly sharpened blade.

"I'll cut my hours back. And I can take the children with me sometimes." She hated the way she sounded, as if she was begging. This wasn't a negotiable deal.

"Sure. And somewhere in there, you might have time to prepare the occasional meal, to go on the occasional family outing, to take the occasional vacation. Good old Ben, he'll raise the kids since I don't have time—"

Her hand was raised before she could think about it. It cracked across his cheek as she screamed, "Stop it!"

His silence was more terrifying than the spew of hateful words.

She reached out to apologize, to comfort, but he spun away from her touch. "Ben, I—"

"Get away from me." There was no heat behind it, simply a weary plea. "Leave me alone."

* * *

Jillian opened her apartment door at Marina's second knock. Behind her was a tall, blond Viking of a man who looked less than thrilled at the interruption.

"Hi, Marina, what— My God! What's happened to you?" Jill reached out and embraced her as she stood sobbing on the doorstep.

She'd been driving aimlessly for hours, sitting in a park until it had grown too cold to bear. She'd intended to be brave, to matter-of-factly ask if she could stay in Jill's spare room, but suddenly the words wouldn't come. She sat in a miserable, sodden heap in Jill's living room, dully watching the cheerfully blinking lights of Jill's enormous Christmas tree as her sister dispatched the Viking with callous haste. Then Jillian put on a pot of water before returning with a giant box of tissues.

Jillian snatched a tissue from the box and blotted at Marina's tears. "Tell Jill, honey. Tell me what's wrong. What's he done to you?"

At the thought of the "he" to whom Jill referred, a fresh torrent of tears cascaded down her cheeks. "I'm pregnant," she blurted. "And Ben doesn't want the baby."

"Ben doesn't want..." Jillian's delighted expression hardened into something murderous. "How inconvenient for him." She sprang to her feet and strode over to her coat closet, yanking out the first garment she laid hands on and stuffing her arms into the sleeves. "Bastard. Lousy, stinking bastard. Just wait. If he thinks for one instant he can trifle with *my sister* and then dump her like a hot potato when he knocks her up, he can damn well think again. I'll cut off his lousy little—''

''Jill!'' Marina jumped up and dragged her away from the door. ''No. That won't solve anything. You don't understand.''

Jillian stood stiffly, resisting Marina's efforts to drag her away from the door. ''Then explain it. Make me understand why Ben doesn't want the baby.''

Marina swallowed. Her head was pounding from the tears she'd shed and she only wanted to curl up in a ball and ignore the world, but she had to talk to Jillian. Her sister was as enraged as Marina had ever seen her, and if she went after Ben now, things could only get worse.

Tentatively she tugged at Jill's arm again. ''Come sit with me? I need a friend, not a protector.''

The tension held for another minute, then Jillian sighed and her body relaxed. ''Sorry. It's gotten to be a habit since your accident.'' She tossed the coat aside and walked back to the couch with Marina. ''Okay. I promise not to rush out and kill him. Yet. Explain.''

It was harder to talk about Carrie as a separate being, a person deceased, than she'd anticipated. ''You know Ben's first wife was a homemaker?'' she began.

Jillian nodded, a glimmer of understanding dawning in her eyes.

Marina started there and told her sister as much as she could of the impasse at which she and Ben found themselves. It was surprisingly cathartic—she'd never had a sister, or even a friend so close. Ben had provided all those needs from the time she'd been in college.

"So what are you going to do now?" Jillian asked when she'd finished her recitation.

Marina shrugged, her eyes filling again. "I'm not Carrie Bradford. I wouldn't be happy if I gave up my work, and ultimately that would destroy my marriage." Her voice quavered. "There's no way to resolve it. The only thing I know to do is to get out of Ben's life before we tear each other apart. I want this baby, even if he doesn't. And I'm going to keep it, no matter what."

Ten

Ten

Ben turned his head and looked at the digital clock face glowing on his nightstand: 4:43 in the morning.

Damn her! How could she have left like that? Without even a note to tell him where she was headed. Guilt twisted his gut as he heard himself hurling his final words at her. *Get away from me. Leave me alone.*

She'd taken him literally.

He'd been so shocked by her revelation, so stunned, that he'd never even heard her leave. When his mother had called to ask who was picking up Jennie, he'd realized it was dinnertime and Marina was gone.

He'd tried the store. No answer.

No answer at Jillian's, either. Where else could she

be? She couldn't be at her old house next door; they'd had all the utilities disconnected when she'd moved in with him.

He'd picked up Jennie and spent the evening entertaining her, holding his fears at bay. He'd expected her to walk in the door any minute. But after Jennie had been put to bed, it had been impossible to hold back the nightmare images...graphic images of the last time he'd lost her, when he'd believed beyond doubt that she was gone from him forever.

Thinking of her possibly hurt, lying alone somewhere... He'd gone to bed and lain tensely as the hours ticked past, wondering where she'd gone.

She'd be back. He had to believe that or his life wouldn't be worth living anymore. Once he'd been left without her, and every day had been shadowed by grief and loneliness, relieved only by the bright miracle of the child they'd made together.

But Jennie didn't belong to him in the same sense Carrie had, in the way he'd belonged to the woman he loved. With every year that passed, Jennie would grow less dependent. Someday he'd have to step back and free her to live her own life.

And he'd be alone.

Like his mother had been alone all her life, struggling to rear a child. Oh, he had some distinct advantages. The money issue wouldn't consume his waking hours as it had his mother's. But deep inside, he knew he wasn't as strong as his mother had been. He couldn't spend the rest of his life alone as she had, striving to make a good life for a child. Deep inside, Ben Bradford was a quivering coward.

She had to come home. Didn't she see how much he needed her?

Before he'd met her, he'd always felt isolated from the world. Even his mother, much as he loved her, hadn't filled the void in his heart.

He could remember coming home to a dark apartment as a schoolboy, completing his homework alone because his mother barely got back in time to throw together a meager supper. As he'd grown older, he'd prepared those meals himself.

He could still recall the despair he felt when he'd opened every cupboard in the sparse kitchen and found nothing—*nothing*—he could fix for dinner. And the expression on his mother's face at the end of the day when she propped her feet up on the hassock in front of the worn rocker in their tiny living room. There was no joy in her eyes, simply the knowledge that in a few short hours she'd leave again to spend more than half a day at whatever jobs she currently held. The only time her gaze ever lit up was when it chanced upon him.

Sometimes he'd almost hated his father for dying.

And he'd sworn, since he was old enough to remember, he'd sworn that his family would never face such a hand-to-mouth existence. His wife would never have to work. A huge insurance policy ensured that, even if he couldn't always be there.

His wife would be able to stay home with the children, lavish on them all the love and attention for which he'd longed as a kid. He could still remember how much he'd envied his best friend. When he'd go to Joey's house after school, there were always fresh-baked cookies waiting to be consumed while they regaled Joey's mom with tales from school. Mouth-watering smells rose from the dinner that was being prepared, and Joey's mother was always smiling and laughing. Hell, she even *sang.*

Ben's mother never sang. She did smile when he told her about the things that happened to him at school, but she was so exhausted that half the time she fell asleep in the rocker before he'd finished.

One time—he must've been about nine—she'd gotten a terrible cold that seemed to hang on for months. He still remembered lying awake at night hearing her deep cough and wondering if he could do enough odd jobs for the neighbors to earn some money to take her to the doctor. *Nine years old, for God's sake.*

No way were his kids ever going to know that feeling of worry over what would happen to them if their mother got ill, or was late getting home, or lost her job. Was it so terrible to want to give his family all those things he'd missed out on as a kid?

It wasn't that he didn't love his mother. He'd loved her fiercely, still did. She'd made sacrifice after sacrifice for him. And she'd never have to worry about finances again. He'd taken care of that.

Slowly he sat up and swung his legs over the edge of the big oak bed. Marina was just trying to punish him. They would talk again when they'd both calmed down and he'd make her see how insane this whole notion was of trying to run a business while juggling two small children and a household.

Two small children. The phrase sounded odd. An insistent whisper of excitement pierced the righteous anger he'd nursed all night. *Another baby!* Abrupt, unexpected tears stung his eyes. He hadn't thought he'd ever have this chance again. He *had* to make Marina understand how foolish this work notion of hers was. If she pushed herself too hard, she might harm herself or the baby.

Full of a new determination, he stood and pulled on a pair of sweatpants and a T-shirt. After a workout on the rowing machine and a quick shower, it would be time to try calling Jillian's again. He'd bet his last dollar she knew where Marina was. Too bad if he woke her.

At six-fifteen, Ben punched out the digits of Jillian's telephone number.

It rang five times before her sleepy voice said, "Hello?"

"Where's Marina?"

There was an odd click and he realized the connection had been broken. He swore mildly as he pressed the redial button. What a time for the phone service to go on the blink.

The second time she answered, he got cut off again.

The third time he tried, Jill didn't say, "Hello." Instead, she picked up the phone, said, "Don't call here again, Ben," and replaced the receiver on her end with a bang.

He was astounded. The phone hadn't been the problem at all. Jillian had been hanging up on him. Infuriated, he threw the portable phone across the room in a rare display of temper. It hit the wall with a sharp thud and crashed to the floor in three pieces.

Damned interfering witch. Now he was positive she knew where Marina was.

He wanted to jump in his car and go roaring over to her house, to confront her and demand to know Marina's whereabouts. He had the keys in his hand before he realized he couldn't leave Jennie. Chagrined, frustrated and furious, he sank down at the kitchen table. The keys clattered to the floor as he plunged both hands deep into his hair. What was he going to do?

Fury wouldn't work with Jillian. As he calmed himself with deep, steady breaths, he knew aggression wasn't the solution. The woman had the temperament of a tiger when it came to protecting her sister. If he wanted to find Marina, he'd have to pour on the charm. Sighing, he rose from the chair and went to make breakfast before he woke Jennie...who was sure to pitch a fit when she found out Marina wasn't here.

He was right. After dropping a tearful toddler off at his mother's, he drove to the store. He arrived at Kids' Place just before nine and parked right along the street, expecting that he'd be in and out quickly. Even if it was Christmas Eve, he still had to work for half a day, and he hoped Jillian wouldn't be difficult. The minute he saw her flip over the Closed sign and unlock the door, he was out of his car and into the shop.

His gaze scanned the store as Jillian turned to face him. He'd been hoping Marina would be here, but it was still a bit early; she didn't usually come in before nine.

"Jill!" He adopted his heartiest tone as she stopped and turned to see who had entered the shop already.

She advanced toward him, and he saw the set expression on her face long before she got close, but it was the look in her eyes that startled him as she drew near. Loathing. Venom. Bottled rage.

"May I help you?" Her tone was an icy contrast to the cheery carols playing on the shop's music system.

"I'm looking for Marina. What time is she coming in?" He didn't quite know how to handle this woman. Jillian had always been flirtatious, warm and friendly, without giving him any real hint of a come-on. When she'd found out he was serious about Marina, she hadn't disguised her pleasure.

"She's not." Jill's voice was brisk, but it didn't quite hide the note of gloating satisfaction. "May I give her a message?"

"Dammit, Jillian!" He knew it was a mistake to let her get to him, but *he needed Marina.* "I know you've seen her. Do you think I'm stupid?"

There was a contemplative silence, just long enough for him to hope she'd overlooked the opening, but no such luck. She smiled, but there was malice rather than humor in it. "I couldn't have found a more accurate label if I'd searched the dictionary." Then her sugary-sweet tone changed and he was appalled at the force of her fury. "On second thought, I rescind that. Stupid doesn't begin to cover what I think of you. My sister wasn't looking for a man when you finagled your way into her life. She'd just lost the only man she ever loved and her memories of him, as well. Then she found you and for a while you conned us both."

She stepped toward him and he tensed, sure she was about to attack. "Jillian, you don't understand—"

"Oh, I understand, all right."

She put both hands flat against his chest and shoved him back a pace. He fought his fury, wanting to tell her the truth about Carrie-Marina so fiercely that he could barely restrain himself. Only the knowledge that Marina would never forgive him kept him from slapping Jill in the face with the fact that her sister had been his wife far longer than she'd ever known Jillian.

But Jillian was unaware of his mental turmoil. "She was thrilled about this baby. *Thrilled.* It was the one thing that would have made her life complete. She thought you loved her, that you'd be as delighted about another child to love as she was to become Jennie's mother. But, no! You only want a replacement for the first paragon you married. Well, let me tell you something, you arrogant jackass, Marina doesn't need you. She loved you, she wanted to spend her life with you, but she's not some wax doll you can manipulate to suit yourself.''

Her lip curled. ''Get out of my shop.''

Desperation mixed with his rising ire. ''Jillian, I love her. I want to work things out. I want Marina and the baby.''

''On your terms. Get out.'' Her voice was as implacable as her face. One hand reached for the telephone on the wall. ''You have five seconds before I call the police. A harassment charge might upset some of your clients a bit.''

He hesitated.

She began to punch numbers.

Muttering a vicious curse, Ben turned and slammed out. Not knowing what else to do, he drove to his office.

The morning was hellish. All he could think of was the deadly sound of Jillian's voice tearing his hopes into shreds. He'd been wrong. Why was it so easy to see it now? He loved Marina. Yes, the experience she'd undergone had altered her irrevocably. She was a different person than Carrie had been—and he'd refused to face it. Any other man would have been so thankful to have gotten a second chance that the job issue would have been a minor adjustment.

He had a difficult time returning the holiday sentiments of his exuberant co-workers as they closed the office at noon. In the car, he switched off the radio with an irritated flick of his wrist. If he heard one more Christmas carol, he'd smash the damned thing into smithereens. The whole way home, he prayed that Marina's car would be in the driveway when he arrived.

But it wasn't.

He didn't know what to do next. Call the police and file a missing-person's report? Make their problems public? He didn't think she'd changed in her dislike of having her privacy invaded. She'd absolutely hate that. Besides, Jillian would be only too happy to tell them that Marina had left of her own free will.

He got out of the car and started toward the house when something on the lawn of her house caught his eye. Unable to credit what he was seeing, he walked slowly across the grass until he was standing directly in front of it.

For Sale.

The realty sign mocked him. Oh, they'd talked about selling the house, but they hadn't done anything about it. He was positive the sign hadn't been there yesterday. His hopes shriveled inside his chest; he could actually feel his heart squeezing tighter and tighter, clenching in pain. *She'd left him for good.*

Moving like an old man, he dragged himself back to his own house. He entered through the garage door and came into the family room. He would go pick up Jennie and pretend to be ecstatic about Santa coming tonight. He deliberately shut out everything else, focusing only on Jennie's excitement about Santa. He couldn't let his little girl down—it gave him a reason to keep moving through the pain.

How he'd explain to Jennie that Marina wouldn't be back—*don't think about her!*

The Christmas tree twinkled merrily as Marina's collection of iridescent glass ornaments caught the sunlight streaming in the windows. He could barely stand the sight of it. Cloud wandered into the room and wound around his ankles; absently he picked her up and rubbed her soft white fur against his cheek. "Where's your mistress?" he asked her softly.

But the cat didn't answer.

Still holding her, he walked into the foyer, heading for the bedroom and a change of clothes. The sight of the boxes stopped him in his tracks; the cat slipped from his hands. Small boxes, large boxes, boxes of all shapes and sizes were stacked carefully in a corner of the foyer, all neatly closed and taped. Marina must have come in and done this earlier today while he was working.

So she really was leaving. *Oh, God, how can I live without you?*

Aimlessly he wandered into Jennie's room, seeking solace, craving comfort for the hurt in his heart. He sank down on the edge of Jennie's bed and picked up a battered-looking stuffed monkey who'd shared Jennie's bed since she was old enough to reach for it. It had been her constant companion in the days right after Carrie's death. Convulsively he clutched it to his chest, then his gaze fell on something lying on the floor by the bed.

He recognized it immediately as he bent to pick up the book of children's poems. It was the one Marina had given Jennie for her birthday, one he'd read many times in the weeks since. Jennie loved it almost as much as she loved Marina.

His big hands trembled and fumbled as he opened the cover and read the inscription on the flyleaf:

To the sweetest little girl in my whole world. All my love on your second birthday, Marina.

With an index finger that shook, he gently traced her flowing script.

Jennie demanded he read Marina's writing every time he read the book. The familiar words hit him like a knockout punch delivered in the final round of a prizefight.

In my whole world…

Guilt and despair surrounded him, suffocating him with every breath. What a self-righteous, small-minded chauvinist he'd been. No wonder she'd left. She should have hit him over the head on her way out the door—maybe it would have shaken the self-ishness loose.

His hands closed into fists and he pressed his knuckles almost violently against his eyes.

He and Jennie *were* her whole world. How could he have doubted it? She was devoted to her family. Never once had she permitted her work to interfere with anything important to their well-being. He re-membered the day he'd come down with the flu. She hadn't hesitated to call Jillian and arrange for time off. Jennie had gone to the shop with her for a while that day, and on several other occasions.

She loved her work. He'd seen her helping a new

grandmother find the perfect baby gift, had watched her pore over the new books and decide which ones to order, had even helped her take inventory one Saturday when she'd been shorthanded. It wasn't just an income, it wasn't just a job. *She loved it.*

She'd grown and changed since the accident. She was more self-assured, more confident and capable. Kids' Place had been good for her. Having a niche of her own, other than simply being Ben Bradford's wife or Jennie's mother, had been good for her.

The old Carrie never would have stood up to him. She'd have been quietly miserable and he'd have been upset and dissatisfied without knowing what was wrong. The new Carrie—Marina—had seen his inflexibility and recognized that he would smother her...and that the inevitable demise of their love would damage Jennie if they played it out.

But she'd been wrong about one thing. He could change. And he would. For her. Because he couldn't live the rest of his life without her. What had seemed so insurmountable yesterday required only a shift of perception to be overcome.

Marina was right. Their lives could include her career without detriment to any member of their family. Even with a baby. Their children wouldn't grow up feeling that their mother had no time for them. Marina would never let that happen.

The baby... Her eyes had shouted her joy and excitement yesterday afternoon. If he'd been thinking, he'd have known right away what had her so tickled. And he'd have responded with equal joy.

The only problems with her career were in his mind. He'd driven her away, and it was up to him to convince her to come home. He'd—

"Ben?"

He snatched his hands away from his eyes and jumped to his feet. *She was back!* His heart leapt and began to beat violently, slamming against his ribs almost painfully as he realized that his second chance could come sooner than he'd expected. Her footsteps drew nearer as she came down the hall, then she was standing in Jennie's bedroom doorway.

"Ben." She looked everywhere but at him. "I'm sorry to intrude. I came to pick up some of my things."

"Where are you going?" Her blond beauty was as stunning as ever, but her blue eyes were haunted. It was all he could do to force his voice out. He was deathly afraid she'd leave again before he could tell her how wrong he'd been.

"I found an apartment that will let me have the animals. I'll look for a house later." She sighed and seemed to gather herself. Her voice was even softer when she spoke next. "I'm sorry. I'm sorry I barged back into your life—" She broke off and her shoulders heaved. "You'd have been better off to finish your grieving and move on. I promise I'll respect whatever decision you make about Jennie. I realize that I have no legal claim to visitation rights. Please, just let her know…let her know how much I love her."

He tried to speak then, but she cut him off with a

palm raised to stop him. "I have to go. I only want to tell you how sorry I am that I—I haven't lived up to your expectations. I won't ask you to have anything to do with this baby. I know you didn't want it to be like this." Tears were running down her cheeks and she swiped at them with a trembling hand.

As always, her tears undid him. He was beside her before he was aware of moving. Tenderly he put his arms around her and pressed her head into his shoulder. "Shh. Don't cry. You know I can't take it when you cry."

She lifted her head and offered him a valiant, lopsided smile through the tears as she struggled free. "I know. I'm sorry. I'll get the things I can't do without and take the animals. I can come back one day next week for the—"

"No."

"What?" She drew away from his hands.

He tried again. This time he'd request, not demand. "What I meant was, you don't have to take your things anywhere."

"Yes, I do. I need some of them."

Was she deliberately misinterpreting his words? He drew a nervous breath as his stomach jittered. The next few minutes of his life might be the most important he'd ever live through. "Marina, don't go," he blurted when she opened her mouth again.

Her light eyebrows rose but he didn't give her a chance to speak.

"I want the baby. I want you." His throat closed up and he spun away, afraid it was too late, that he couldn't take back the hurt he'd inflicted yesterday, that she didn't love him anymore. He'd already been given a second chance...he didn't deserve a third.

"What are you saying?" Her voice was a bare thread of sound, as if she was afraid to leap to conclusions.

He took a deep breath and turned to face her. "I'm saying that I was wrong. I didn't want you to work because I was afraid. Afraid you'd love your job more than me. My lifelong goal has been to be able to provide for my family. It was threatening when I found that you really didn't need me."

"Oh, Ben." Marina shook her head helplessly. "Don't you know I'll always need you? That my love for you isn't dependent on how much money you make or whether we have a spacious home? I'd love you even if we had to struggle to keep a roof over our heads."

She advanced toward him and took his face between her small palms. "I'd want this baby even if we didn't know how to stretch our budget to make ends meet—because it's a precious, living symbol of our love." Her eyes were luminous and compelling as she whispered, "I loved you enough to come back to you. You are part of my heart."

He wanted to raise his arms, to clutch her to him and accept her gift of unconditional love, but the guilt that had been festering within him for months rose inexorably.

"I don't deserve another chance," he said, dropping his head in dull shame. "Knowing we'd never have more babies was a shock. And I behaved like a self-centered child. If I had been watching Jennie more closely that day, you'd never have—"

Her palm over his mouth cut him off and her voice was passionate. "Oh, Ben, you can't blame yourself for that. Have you been thinking this way since the accident?"

When he gave a barely perceptible nod, she closed her eyes and inhaled sharply. "My God." Then her eyelids slowly opened again. "I won't let you think that. It wasn't your fault."

"But—"

"But nothing." Her voice was strong and firm. Somehow he felt as if their roles had been reversed and he was the one taking strength from her. "We might not have been communicating, but we were every bit as vigilant about Jennie's safety as we are today. Accidents happen. Children are unpredictable. The accident was no more your fault than it was mine."

He hadn't realized how badly he'd needed to hear those words. *It wasn't your fault.* Slowly the clump of guilt inside him began to dissolve. "I wanted to talk to you," he said. "I wanted to tell you I was sorry...but the words weren't there. I like to think I'd have gotten past the self-pity and reached out to you. I knew you were hurting, too."

The lines of stress in her face had eased. "If I hadn't been killed, we'd have had to deal with our feelings eventually," she said. "We'd have faced our problems and worked them out like any other couple.''

He could see her eyes change as the incongruity of the words struck her and she chuckled. He smiled, too, feeling lighter than he had in months. ''Please come back to me,'' he said. ''I want you to be happy, to enjoy your shop. I know that it will never replace me. Your commitment to us and our family exceeds anything else in your life.''

He lowered his head, needing to seal his plea with a physical sign of his love. She met him eagerly, winding her arms around his neck and lifting her lips for his.

When he lifted his head, they were both breathing raggedly.

''We'll start hunting for a housekeeper tomorrow,'' he vowed. ''We'll need someone who likes animals, someone who will devote most of their time to our children and fit in some housekeeping during naps and the times we have the kids—''

''Ben.'' Marina put her hand over his mouth. Then she giggled, running her palms along his lean cheeks, enjoying the bristly stubble of his beard. ''Tomorrow's Christmas Day. I'm afraid you'll have to wait a bit to begin this manhunt.''

''Womanhunt,'' he corrected her, unfazed. ''I want a rosy-cheeked, cookie-baking grandmother who will sing nursery rhymes and push swings.''

She shook her head ruefully. ''My, my. You do have definite opinions, don't you?''

''You mean you haven't noticed?'' He mimed rapping himself in the head with a fist. Then he said, "Speaking of definite opinions, I think your sister's after my head on a platter. Tell me what I have to do to get back in her good graces."

Marina's eyes softened. "Seeing us together, happy about the baby, should do it. Jill doesn't talk about her problems, but I think she's wrestling with her own demons and you stirred up some bad memories."

"Stirred up?" His echo was wry. "I felt like I'd tossed a match into a drum of kerosene."

"Jill does tend to react decisively," she said, laughing again. Then she took his hand and placed it over her abdomen as she smiled up at him. "In a few more weeks, you'll be able to feel him moving."

"Him?"

"This one's going to be a boy."

"I know better than to argue with someone who has a direct pipeline to heaven." He rubbed his nose gently against hers. "But just in case, let's decide on a girl's name, too."

"Are you sure you want to waste time brainstorming names right now?" She moved her hips against him provocatively. "I can think of a better way to spend the next few minutes before we pick up Jennie."

"So can I." Ben slid his hands up under the loose sweater she wore. "And I intend to spend many, many minutes in the rest of our years together showing you how much I love you."

She smiled and her head fell back as he bent to nuzzle at her neck. In the back of her mind echoed words from her extraordinary journey. *Someday you'll understand...you and Ben.*

Love had given her a second chance at this lifetime. Surely love would carry them together into the next.

* * * * *

American HEROES
AGAINST ALL ODDS

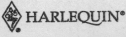 HARLEQUIN®   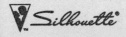 Silhouette®

Please address questions and book requests to: Harlequin Reader Service U.S.: 3010 Walden Ave.,
P.O. Box 1325, Buffalo, NY 14269 CAN.: P.O. Box 609, Fort Erie, Ont. L2A 5X3   PAHGEN

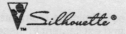

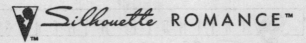